WINDFALL

ONE

by

Jeff Ross

CONTENTS

1

BULLETS ARE FLYING

Jeremy Staymour glanced at his watch. Eight AM. He had been building a portfolio for a major client for two hours. He stopped, rubbed his eyes, and rolled his chair back in a panic. *I've got to finish this report!*

Beads of sweat lined his forehead while he sat and stared. Suddenly, something lured him to his office window. A silhouette in a business suit peered out of an adjacent building—a tall man with a hat and binoculars.

Not wanting to be spotted, Jeremy backed away from the window. Then he edged closer to the window casing to get a better look. He spotted a second man talking on a cell and straining to see across the alley.

Both men turned away sharply when they realized Jeremy was on to them. The binocular man reappeared—this time he was staring through the crosshairs of a gun scope aimed at Jeremy's office. Jeremy pulled back sharply from the window and his mind went into overdrive. He tried to rationalize, but nothing was clear. Don't panic! Stay away from the window.

Heart pounding, he crawled army-style to the door and looked down the hall—it was clear! Get me the hell out of here! He scampered down the hall, looking for anything out of the ordinary. There was nothing. His mind shifted to the business contacts he made the day before. The deal...the money...it all sounded great. But there was one problem—it was illegal, big-time illegal. Not worth going to jail over!

Jeremy's mind was on overload. He blinked and shook his head abruptly to snap out of it. Focus! He took a few more steps and then it occurred again. His mind recalled the strange men in the other building...he envisioned being clubbed by a gang of thugs in a dark alley.

He rushed to the elevator entry and waited. Thirty seconds...forty-five seconds. It seemed like an eternity for the doors to open! The floor numbers flashed at a snail's pace above the doors—26, 25, 24. He slammed the button a few more times. "Come on...come on," he ranted. Finally, the doors opened and he hopped inside. He pushed the Lobby button. Two seconds, three seconds...The doors finally closed.

The elevator descended and finally came to a stop. As the doors inched open, the impatient Jeremy slithered out and stormed through the crowded lobby toward the revolving doors to Race Street. He maneuvered through the hundreds of Fountain Square party-goers from a large convention.

Jeremy sidestepped a homeless man. *Get out of the way, man…I need to find my car!* His Nissan was parked in the remodeled City Garage. Jeremy darted through the crowd and made it to Vine Street. While only a few steps from the garage entrance, he froze. It all happened so quickly. There was a loud screech of tires and the burning smell of rubber, then a dark-colored Beemer appeared out of nowhere, storming wildly down the street. A group of onlookers stared in bewilderment at the commotion.

Two old-style rifles poked through the car windows and sprayed a barrage of bullets. Jeremy had virtually no time to defend himself. He ducked slightly and raised his forearm to shield his face, but it was too late. He was already struck in the neck and shoulder, causing him to stagger a few steps before clumsily dropping to the sidewalk. While lying there, Jeremy felt a stinging pain above his right eyebrow where another bullet had grazed the side of his head. He reached for his throat and gasped for air.

The BMW's horn blared during the getaway. The car blew through a red light and weaved through heavy traffic. When the smoke cleared, the frightened homeless man hobbled across the street and disappeared into a nearby alley. The shocked onlookers on the Square were motioning to one another, but no one offered to help the injured Jeremy.

———

Seconds later, an attractive woman jogger appeared. She was a brunette in her late twenties, wearing a sweat suit and headband. The woman looked around cautiously and ensured that the fleeing car was safely out of sight. As she bent down, she saw a man grimacing in pain and struggling to breathe. Warm blood oozed from his wounds and saturated his collar.

"Hang in there, buddy…keep fighting," she whispered in his ear.

Trying to remain calm, the woman stood and untied her sweatshirt from her waist. Then she bent to her knees and loosened the man's tie.

"Uhhhh," Jeremy gasped as he rolled slowly on the pavement.

"Shhhh," she said, putting two fingers over his lips. "Don't try to talk…you're going to be just fine." She wadded her sweatshirt and formed a pillow for his head. She spoke a few more words of encouragement and prayed that he would not die in her arms.

Stop the bleeding…direct pressure! she recalled from a CPR class. She wrapped the sleeve of the sweatshirt around Jeremy's neck wound in an attempt to slow the bleeding. Direct pressure to the wound, she repeated.

The woman tied the sweatshirt sleeve securely on the neck wound. She nervously looked down Fifth Street for more help, but only a few bums were on one corner and the business people were on the other. Both groups were observing the commotion, but no one offered any assistance.

The jogger's hands and clothes were drenched with Jeremy's blood. She prayed that she could save his life. Still searching for solutions, the jogger found a headband in her pocket and stretched it carefully around the man's bleeding head. The passing minutes seemed like an eternity. Finally, an ambulance roared around the corner and skidded to a stop. Three paramedics jumped out of the emergency vehicle and ran across the Square to the spot where Jeremy was lying.

"Can you tell me what happened?" a woman paramedic asked, while two others worked on Jeremy.

"I was jogging when a dark-colored car flew by here and men were shooting from the car windows. There were so many bullets ricocheting that I almost got hit myself!"

"And then what?" a male paramedic asked.

"When the coast was clear, I ran over to help."

The jogger answered a few more questions and was thanked by the paramedics for her help. She bent down and spoke a few more words of encouragement in Jeremy's ear. "Remember what I told you... You're going to be fine now."

Within minutes, the paramedics strapped Jeremy to a backboard and carefully loaded him into the life squad.

———

Ricki Valentes had just won thirty-nine million dollars in the multi-state lottery. So she and her boyfriend, Daniel Flarity, needed to invest the windfall. They performed a thorough search for Certified Financial Planners and decided on a company called JTST Investments. While researching the company, Daniel remembered Jeremy Staymour from high school, where they played football together. Staymour went on to be a Financial Advisor and later formed his own company called JTST Investments. Recently, Daniel read an article in the Wall Street Journal that touted the excellent growth of JTST over the last five years.

Based on Daniel's research and since he knew Staymour, he convinced Ricki to go with JTST. Ricki agreed, and they had a long telephone conversation with Jeremy the previous week.

"Mr. Staymour told us last week that he had already selected the investments and that everything could be done electronically," Ricki said.

"Yes, he did," Daniel recalled. Ricki pulled out her iPad, completed her personal information, and confirmed the trade details.

Two hours later, she received a text notification that read:

Ricki Valentes – Trade setup…8:18 PM.
$30,502,000

Ricki was thrilled that the gigantic trade was in progress and that her lottery winnings would soon be in the market. The actual trades would occur within twenty-four to forty-eight hours.

Ricki and Daniel didn't have the television on when they invested the fortune on the JTST Investments website. They didn't realize that the owner, Jeremy Staymour, was stricken by multiple bullets and was fighting for his life.

2

JEREMY IS RUSHED TO THE HOSPITAL

The Paramedics wheeled Jeremy into the Emergency Ward of County Memorial Hospital. The medical staff ran alongside the gurney. The paramedics had already wrapped a large white bandage around the top of his head.

"Quick, get him over here!" Nurse Laura Williams yelled to the hospital staff. They edged the gurney a little closer to the medical equipment.

"Ahhhh," Jeremy moaned in pain as he struggled to focus.

"Just relax," the resident urged, "we'll take good care of you." The adrenaline was flowing for John Behringer, a new resident on only his second hospital assignment. Within minutes, the ER physician, Dr. Barry Campbell, busted through the swinging doors to examine the patient. With no time to lose, Behringer rolled the crash cart and defibrillator next to the patient. He grabbed the suture tray in case stitches were necessary.

As the medical staff worked diligently on young Jeremy, there was a crowd of family members waiting anxiously in the waiting room. His sister, Liz, had driven down from Springboro as soon as she heard the news. She was Jeremy's only living relative in his direct family. Jeremy's parents were killed in the late nineties in a tragic car accident in Michigan. The other relatives —a few aunts and uncles from nearby Mason—were also notified of the shooting, and waited alongside her.

"What can you tell me about his injuries? Is he going to make it?" Liz begged the receptionist on the Emergency floor.

"The doctors are doing everything in their power," the receptionist replied.

"But how bad are his injuries?" Liz persisted.

The receptionist walked around the curved counter and put her arm around Liz to console her. Liz's boyfriend, Heath, had left work early and was in the waiting room.

"Please take a seat here," the receptionist said as she took Liz by the arm to the waiting room. "I'll fill you in as soon as I hear something."

Liz saw Heath waiting and quickly ran over to hug him. Consumed with anguish over her brother's trauma, she turned to her boyfriend for comfort. "I just can't believe this has happened!" she lashed out. Tears streaming from her face, she reached for the wadded tissue in her pocket. "Who would shoot Jeremy?"

Heath rubbed her back and gently patted her on the shoulder. Finally, he convinced her to sit down. Then he bent down and kissed her gently on the forehead. "It'll be okay, honey…the doctors are with him," he said. Liz hugged him again and repeated softly.

"Why…who would do this to my brother? He wouldn't hurt a fly."

Heath hugged and consoled Liz for the next several minutes without them speaking another word. It was not apparent to either of them who would have done this. *Why would anyone want to harm Jeremy?*

Thirty minutes later, the hospital receptionist motioned to get Liz's attention.

"Excuse me, Ms. Staymour?"

"Yes?"

"Could you please come here for a moment to complete some paperwork?"

Liz wiped her eyes and waved to the receptionist. "I'll be right back," she whispered to Heath as they released hands. She walked over to the reception desk and looked sadly at the woman whose badge read *Sally McNamara.*

"How can I help?" Liz asked.

"I'm so sorry about your brother, but we'll take good care of him."

"Thank you."

"First of all, is this the correct spelling of your last name?"

Liz leaned over the monitor and confirmed that it was.

"And does your brother have medical insurance?"

"I'm sure he does since he owns a company…"

"Oh, really? What company?"

"JTST Investments." She typed it in and then continued.

"Is he married?"

"No…single," Liz answered as she recalled Rachel Miller, Jeremy's former twenty-four-year-old fiancée. Jeremy had caught her fooling around with a pro baseball player in a ritzy Cincinnati hotel room.

"Is your brother allergic to any medication?" the receptionist continued. Liz didn't respond. "Ms. Staymour?"

"Uh…no," Liz answered. "No allergies that I know of."

"That's good. I'll get his medical card when he comes out of the OR," Mrs. McNamara said as she typed some of the preliminary contact information. "Thanks for your help."

When Mrs. McNamara finally looked up from her computer, Liz was still in a daze.

"Ms. Staymour, are you okay?"

"Uh, sure," Liz mumbled. She slowly turned and rejoined Heath in the waiting room.

About twenty minutes later, a police detective approached the reception desk. Liz struggled to make out what he was saying, but she only saw him pull out a small notebook. After a few minutes, Mrs.

McNamara pointed and the detective walked in Liz's direction. "Excuse me, Ms. Staymour..."

Liz finished wiping the tears from her eyes and turned toward the detective.

"Yes sir," she answered politely.

"Hello, I'm Detective Lankford," he said as he shook hands with Liz and then Heath. "May I sit down?"

Liz nodded and scooted closer to Heath on the padded bench. Lankford pulled open his notebook and scribbled a few more notes.

"I'm sorry about your brother, Ms. Staymour."

"Thanks for your concern, Detective."

Lankford waited a few seconds then continued. "Any idea who may have done this?" he began. "Did Jeremy have any enemies that you know of?"

"Can't this wait, Detective?" Heath interjected. "She's still very ups—"

"No...it's okay," Liz commented while motioning at Heath. She wiped a tear from her eye and redirected her attention toward Lankford.

"Thanks, Ms. Staymour...I'll keep it short."

Noticing that the detective was starting to feel awkward, Liz continued. "I'm at a complete loss, Detective. My brother is the nicest guy you'd ever meet. I just can't believe he was shot. Nobody would hurt Jeremy!"

"This may seem uncomfortable, Ms. Staymour, but I have to ask you anyway…did your brother either *use or sell* drugs?"

Liz's eyes widened with anger. "No, not Jeremy! My brother was in the top five percent in his class, National Honor Society, football star, the whole works."

"Did he gamble…or owe anybody money?

"Not that I know of, and I'd be shocked if he did," she answered.

Their conversation was interrupted when two paramedics wheeled in a mother and a twelve-year-old boy who were involved in a serious car accident on the highway. Some interns and nurses ran over to assist in rolling the boy past Admitting. A few visitors stopped and stared at the commotion as the ER doctor shouted instructions to the medical staff.

When the commotion subsided, Detective Lankford redirected his questioning to Liz. Seeing Liz's strife, Heath interrupted again.

"Detective…can we do this another time? She's devastated about her brother."

Lankford rose from the bench and closed his notepad. He slid a business card to Liz and asked her to call the station in the morning. Seeing Lankford head out the door, Mrs. McNamara ended her call and motioned for Liz to come over.

"Ms. Staymour, I have an update on your brother's condition."

3

OH JEREMY, PLEASE WAKE UP

Daniel Flarity was originally from Seattle but moved to the Midwest five years ago when he was in college. Playing pool in his basement, he sank the three ball and walked around the table for his next shot—a combination shot off the eight ball. Solid shot! Then he paused and glanced at the big screen TV. The podcaster was interviewing a local investor on some of the hottest ETFs.

Daniel grabbed his cell and typed some notes about a little-known diversification strategy. As the news anchor probed and the investor provided advice, Daniel was fascinated with investing. *I think I can double my money!*

Seconds later, Ricki walked down the steps. She was wearing Daniel's *Cocomo Joe* T-shirt and cutoff jeans shorts. Ricki swayed and danced suggestively to the slow music playing in the background.

"Would you like a sip of my margarita?"

"Um…tastes good," he commented, smiling at his pretty girlfriend. He adored her big brown eyes and slender figure. He reached up and wrapped his arms around her as they giggled playfully.

The television was still playing in the background.

"Turning now to news," the reporter began, "a businessman was shot in the head and neck today on Fountain Square. A BMW stormed wildly through downtown spraying bullets toward a crowd of unsuspecting pedestrians."

Upon hearing this, Daniel pulled away from Ricki's grasp and focused intently on the breaking news. A confused Ricki tugged at Daniel but he resisted again and sat up straight on the sofa. He was absorbed in the story.

An attractive newswoman was under an umbrella on the screen, holding a microphone as she provided the details. "Behind me is County Memorial Hospital, where a man is fighting for his life in the ICU. We are told that the injured man is a businessman who works somewhere on the Square. The Cincinnati police are investigating the incident."

"Are there any leads at this time, Cathy?" the news anchor probed.

"Not yet, Jim. The police are inside the hospital and we believe they are questioning an eyewitness and a family member… but so far, no leads on the shooters or the victim."

"Strange," Daniel mumbled as he continued his fixation on the television.

"What…what is it, honey?" Ricki demanded with a puzzled look.

Daniel stared blankly as the reporters babbled on. He was anxious and confused. *A drive-by shooting in Cincinnati?*

––––––

When Liz Staymour reached the Reception desk of County Memorial, Mrs. McNamara apprised her of the situation.

"One bullet grazed Jeremy's forehead. Another one struck his neck and shoulder."

"Oh my God! What else can you tell me?" Liz asked solemnly.

"The doctors worked feverishly for about forty minutes and Jeremy seemed to be making progress. But at ten this morning, his condition declined. Soon afterward, the trauma caused him to slip into a coma."

Liz couldn't believe her ears. She feared losing her only brother. "A coma…how could he be in a coma?"

"The doctors will be able to give you more details later today," Mrs. McNamara said. 'But you are able to visit him if you'd like." Seconds later, Heath arrived. Liz turned and hugged him.

"Thank goodness you're here, Heath."

They were ready to visit Jeremy when Aunt Lois and Uncle James arrived. Liz quickly apprised them of the situation. They, too, struggled to hold back tears.

"Well, you guys take a seat and make yourself comfortable," Liz said. "We're going up to Jeremy's room."

"Sure," said Aunt Lois. "You and Heath go on up first. We'll wait until you return."

Liz and Heath rode the elevator, rushed down the hallway, and entered Jeremy's room in the ICU. He was intubated and his eyes were open, but glazed. Next to him was a monitor displaying all of his vitals. There was a constant beeping sound in the background.

It was so painful for Liz to see her brother in this condition. Heath remained by the door and signaled for Liz to have alone time with her brother. She walked over to Jeremy and bent down near his face. "Hi, buddy. I'm so glad to see you."

She paused a few seconds to fight off a tear. She said some more, but was unsure if Jeremy could hear or understand her. However, Liz truly believed that Jeremy could sense her in the room.

Liz continued to gaze at her brother's seemingly lifeless face. She shook her head in disbelief and then continued. "I'm right here, Jay. You're *going* to pull through…hang in there, big bro." She sometimes preferred calling him by his nickname, Jay.

Liz whispered a few more words of encouragement and hugged her brother. Then she rose, clenched her fists, and turned in dispair. *Why did this happen? Why must he suffer?*

Seconds later, she pulled a tissue from her purse. She hated seeing her brother like this. Every time she looked at him, Jeremy had the same blank expression on his face—glazed eyes, shallow breathing, and no signs of real life. A state of limbo. Liz paused a moment in reflection and then prayed some more.

The medical definition of a coma is "a form of unconsciousness" and there are many uncertainties with each case. Jeremy's doctors said that there was a twenty percent chance that he would awaken from the coma. "His condition is that of a sleeping person who simply doesn't awaken," the doctors had told her. They went on to say, "Many times, comatose patients move on to the next stage, a persistent vegetative state."

A lone tear trickled down Liz's cheek. She recalled some childhood memories that she had with her brother when they were young. They were playing pickup basketball games in their teen years. She remembered the day he turned sixteen and got his driver's license.

Having no other siblings, Liz and Jeremy had formed a very close relationship that continued into adulthood—until the day that Jeremy formed JTST Investments. Soon thereafter, Jeremy became obsessed with cost models, compounding, and stock analysis. Soon he would manage people's money. Soon, he gained some multi-million dollar clients and his money obsession began.

After gazing around the room in thought, Liz looked back down at Jeremy. There were no signs of responsiveness in his body—a breathing tube, multiple IVs, and an ECMO machine were sustaining his life. The ECMO machine extracted Jeremy's blood, re-oxygenate it, and returned it to his body. The surgeons were evaluating whether a tracheostomy would be necessary due to Jeremy's throat injury.

Liz just shook her head at the sight of her brother. "Can he hear us?" she asked the doctor who entered the room.

"Probably so," Dr. Kingsbury confirmed. "There have been accounts of coma patients hearing sounds and forming some words while comatose."

"Well that's encouraging," Liz said.

"Yes, but to be clear, comatose patients rarely respond to external stimuli. However, there is always that chance."

"Is he in any pain?"

"The research is not conclusive on that, however, I don't believe so," Kingsbury answered as he glanced down at Jeremy.

A nurse squirted a clear liquid into Jeremy's eyes to moisten them, then used two fingers to close his eyelids. There was a pause in the conversation before Liz continued questioning the medical staff.

"How long will he be in the coma, doctor?"

"Hard to tell… days, weeks, months."

"But not years?" she pleaded.

"There are no promises," Kingsbury answered. "I just can't rule out anything at this point. We hope there isn't any hemorrhaging in his brain."

Liz was consumed with fear and uncertainty. She wiped her eyes with a tissue and hugged Dr. Kingsbury. Sensing Liz's uneasiness, the doctor wrapped his arms around her and gently rubbed her shoulder. This comforted her for the moment. A few seconds later, Liz lifted her head from the doctor's shoulder and returned her eyes to Jeremy.

How helpless he was. After a few more seconds, she whispered, "I need you to wake up, Jay...please wake up."

4

CAMPFIRE STORIES

The stories continued long after midnight around the campfire. A group of guys were tent camping in a secluded wooded park in southeastern Ohio. The sounds of birds and crickets could be heard through the tall pines lining the evening sky.

Beer cans were littered around each of the camper's chairs as a few of the men finished their steaks. One of the men leaned too far and toppled his lounge chair to the ground. The others roared in laughter as they lofted marshmallows at the drunken man.

As it got later, many wandered to their tents for the evening. Within a half-hour, the only sound was the soft popping of the smoldering campfire. An hour later, a light rain gently touched the tents.

The following morning was an artist's dream. The sun shone brilliantly through the pines. Thousands of tiny, brown needles blanketed the ground, leaving only a few patches of green grass.

Spikes casted his line from a small fishing boat in the pond below the campsite. The light breeze formed gentle ripples across the pond.

"I could stay out here all day!" Spikes commented to a fellow fisherman, LD. He never told anyone his real name, but just went by LD and he was definitely the ringleader.

"Yeah, nothin' could top this," LD yelled joyfully. Fifteen minutes passed without a fish being caught. Finally, Spikes commented, "Hey, did you hear the news yesterday about that investor? Shot in the head while walking out of his office building near the Square."

"Did they kill him?" LD asked.

"The link said he's on life support down at County Memorial," Spikes replied. "And he's in a coma now."

"Damn…are they sure that he isn't a pusher, maybe somebody getting even?"

"No, he's a wealth manager…owns the firm, I think."

Suddenly LD showed a renewed interest. "Oh yeah? Did they mention his name?"

"I want to say Stamen or Stay-something."

"It wasn't Staymour, was it?" LD asked in alarm.

"Yeah, that's it…Jeremy Staymour. Have you heard of him?"

LD stared aimlessly into the water. He suddenly didn't feel like talking.

After a few seconds, Spikes repeated his probing. "LD, have you heard of this guy, Staymour?

"Yeah, and you're not going to believe it—I've got a few ETFs with him—but nothing crazy."

"You're kidding me," Spikes answered with a grin. "I hope he survives, especially for your sake."

"Yeah," LD replied while deep in thought. He didn't want to reveal his real concerns.

Both men cast their rods, reeled, and cast again. Ripples formed steadily on the water. They watched their lines intently, looking for the slightest tugging, hoping for a bite.

"Water temperature's too damn cold," Spikes mumbled as he tried to change the subject.

"Let's keep at it," LD replied as he fought off his sudden worries. "I'm getting some hits." Within minutes, he felt a tug. He snapped his rod back and hooked a largemouth bass.

"Got him!" he bragged as he pulled in a five-pounder.

"You dog!" Spikes kidded.

About twenty minutes later, the sun was heating the water. The fish were biting and both men landed a few more largemouth bass. They trolled around the lake for about an hour more, before finally calling it quits. Spikes cranked up the small outboard motor and cruised over to the shore. As the boat was returning to the shore of the campsite, Leroy was the first to greet them.

"It's about time…we're starving," he poked with a sly smile.

"Stir up the fire!" Spikes yelled.

That evening, the four men sat around the campfire feasting on good food and drink. They shared some interesting solutions to the world's problems—everything from fixing the welfare system to solving world hunger.

The men drank and drank. When they were out of stories or lies, they stumbled to their tents. A half dozen empty lounge chairs and a pile of empty beer cans littered the campsite. Twenty minutes later, only insect noises and the smoldering fire remained.

When he was sure the others were asleep, LD unzipped his tent, stood, and walked over to a nearby tree to relieve himself. Then he turned and quickly perused the campsite once more.

Assuming the others were asleep, he turned and jogged a half mile to the top of the road. He walked a little further into the clearing to get a signal. He surveyed his surroundings, pulled out his cell, and quickly tapped in the number. He kicked some loose dirt while waiting for the call to go through.

———

Buck Martinez was exercising at an all-night health club when his phone sounded. He wiped his brow and answered.

"Yeah."

"Buck…it's me. Did you see the news?"

Martinez paused before continuing. "LD, this is your burner, isn't it?"

"Yeah, and sorry, Buck, for the bad transmission. I'm somewhere in East Jesus on a camping trip…doing some prospecting. The damn mosquitoes are eating me alive," he said while slapping his neck.

"Buck, you're breaking up…"

"No problem," Buck answered, "but let's make this quick."

"Staymour was shot but he lived through it!"

"Okay. I'll tell the guys to lay low for a while."

5

JEREMY GETS A SURPRISE VISITOR

Buck Martinez didn't expect LD to go into detail on a cell. There were strict rules against that—too easy to trace. He wrapped up his call with LD and quickly called Bobby Wainright. *Maybe I can get some information from the track.*

Buck walked through the lobby of the health club and down a narrow hallway to a side exit. Although he was using his burner, he didn't want to be overheard. After a few rings, the call connected.

"Bobby…it's me."

"Hey Buck, I've been meaning to call you. Did you hear about the shooting? Wasn't one of our guys, was it?"

"No, the guy's name was Staymour. Specializes in mutuals, ETFs, and a lot of the big stuff."

"I thought his name sounded familiar," Wainright yelled. He could barely hear over the roar of the passing stock car. The time trials had started late because of rain.

"Anyway," Martinez continued, "LD told me to tell the guys to place as they were directed in the meeting. Everything's gotta line up to make sure the bets go our way."

"You've got it," Wainright answered. "I'll make sure they understand."

"Oh," Bobby continued., "I just got a text from LD... I'm supposed to place third in today's race and fourth next week." He paused a few seconds then continued. "I'll make it look like a shootout and then tap the brake at the last second to make sure I don't win the damn thing!" he said with a grin.

Bobby realized that the huge betting scandal always pays two to three times more than any legit prize money. He paused a few seconds to continue dreaming of a windfall very soon.

Noticing a pause in the conversation, Wainright yelled into the phone. "Buck...are you still there?"

"Huh? Oh, sorry, Bobby...I was distracted. Go on."

"I was just saying that I had a funny feeling about this Staymour character. Something just didn't smell right with the whole JTST arrangement. First he says he's with us and then he gets cold feet? Can't trust a guy like that!"

"Well...don't panic, Bobby. We've been instructed by LD and Kinsey to stay out of the limelight until the smoke clears," Buck emphasized.

———

Jeremy's condition showed a decrease in oxygen to the brain. His pupils maintained the same blank stare. His brain awareness was sketchy at best. Jeremy was known to flinch at certain sounds in the room. There was a chance he could sense people in the room.

Because of Jeremy's high profile and his shooters still being under investigation, the police left nothing to chance. They placed a security guard around the clock at the ICU. Today's guard was a heavyset man named Wilson.

Pacing by Jeremy's door, Wilson was bored. Time seemed to move in reverse. His stomach was growling for the steaks he planned for later. Then, he was pleasantly surprised when a young, pretty nurse walked by.

"Hello, officer," Nurse Curtis said. "Morning, ma'am," he said. Nurse Curtis nodded as she passed. When she entered Jeremy's room, she saw a nurse adjusting the pillow under Jeremy's head.

"Hi, Gail."

"Angie?" the other nurse began. "I thought you were off work today."

"Wasn't supposed to be here, but Lois took a sick day....so I decided to work for her." As she edged closer, Angie squinted to read the name on the patient's wristband. "What's the story with this guy?" she asked curiously.

"Quite a mystery," Gail began. "His name is Jeremy Staymour...some investment guy. Injured in a drive-by shooting on

Fountain Square…poor guy almost bled out but a woman jogger came to his rescue."

"It is a shame," Angie agreed. "Guy's in his late twenties—much too young to be in a coma!" She shook her head in disbelief.

"Yeah, unfortunately in this place they come in all ages."

"Do they know who shot him?" Angie asked with some concern in her voice.

"Not a clue—but I overheard that he works near the Square."

"Really?" Angie commented with increased interest. She bent down to get a closer look at his face. Then gently rubbed his cheek in a circular motion. "He is a cutie, isn't he?"

"Now Angie, you know the rules—no fraternizing with the patients…especially the comatose ones," Gail giggled. She tugged Angie by the arm and they headed for the door.

As the nurses left the room, neither of them recognized the doctor who was entering. He was in his forties, about five-eight, and of medium build. He was somewhat official looking as he wore scrubs, had a stethoscope around his neck, and carried a notebook computer. He also had hospital identification clipped to his pocket.

"Can we help you with anything?" Nurse Curtis asked.

"Thanks, but I'll just be doing a few routine tests," the doctor answered. His medical disguise working perfectly, Edward Kinsey was relieved when the nurses left the room. He waited for less than a minute until their voices completely faded down the hall. Then he turned his full attention to the helpless patient.

Jeremy felt like he was in prison. He was in *la-la* land with no control of his faculties. Wherever he was, he could see nothing or feel nothing. But he could hear faint noises once in a while. *Am I dead? Am I in the afterlife?* Jeremy's brain felt like mush. No coherent thoughts—just glimpses and random images. He heard disjointed words or phrases.

He faintly recalled the two nurses entering the room. He heard one of the nurses call him a cutie. At some point, he heard strange footsteps. Jeremy wasn't sure how he knew it, but his mind warned him *This guy's a phony!*

Even in a comatose state…he *sensed* something terrible. The villain walked to the head of Jeremy's bed and spoke some haunting words. Then he bent over, grabbed a fistful of Jeremy's hair, and pulled abruptly.

"I hope you enjoy your sleep, young Jeremy—it'll certainly be a long one."

No visible response from the patient.

Then Kinsey continued taunting poor Jeremy. "Is there anything you would like to say before we begin here?"

When Jeremy didn't answer, Kinsey glared with daggers at his comatose victim.

"That sure is a sweet little sister of yours," Kinsey said with continued cockiness. He paused a few seconds to savor the moment. Jeremy's heart rate accelerated as indicated by the monitors above his head. Flash, beep. Flash, flash, beep!

That voice sounds familiar…but I just can't place it. Who is this creep and why is he here?

Kinsey continued tormenting. "I just wanted to thank you, Jay boy, for working so hard to accumulate so much wealth…you were brilliant," Kinsey said wryly as he blew a puff of air in Jeremy's face. "We offered you a good deal. Give us a list of five names—your top clients."

Jeremy didn't answer. He couldn't.

Kinsey continued the tormenting, "Now it's time for beddy-bye, little Jay…isn't that what your sister calls you, Jay boy?"

Jeremy's heart was on overload. *Don't bring Liz into this—she has nothing to do with any of this…let me snap out of this nightmare! I don't want to die, you frickin' thug…not now…and not like this!*

———

No one heard Jeremy's plea for help—he couldn't utter a sound. Unlike the movies, no alarms sounded, no doors flew open, and no staff came running to his aid.

Jeremy lay there for what seemed like an eternity—a prolonged silence. The torture of a bedridden man in a coma.

Where did you go? Where are you?! Show your face, and I'll kill you right now!

More silence. Jeremy angled his head toward the direction of his nemesis. But there was nothing. Nothing but a cold and eerie darkness.

6

TAUNTING AND MORE TAUNTING

Even in an unconscious state, Jeremy's mind fought for survival. *Concentrate!* his mind shouted. *Fight this punk! Come on, come on, dammit. Focus, you've got to focus!* But Jeremy's internal compass was in a whirlwind. *If only I could…*and then it happened.

Kinsey connected a tiny bag of a milky poison to Jeremy's import valve. The mystery drug would soon cause convulsions, tremors, and irregular heartbeat. If left untreated, Jeremy's remaining life was down to an hour or less.

Jeremy was not aware of the lethal concoction streaming into his bloodstream. Instead, he drifted miles away. When the bag was empty, Kinsey yanked it off the port and stuffed it in his pocket. He looked around to ensure that no one had entered the room. With an evil smirk, Kinsey glanced down at his helpless victim and mocked him. *That was WAY too easy, Jay-boy!*

———

Officer Wilson returned to his post in front of Jeremy Staymour's hospital room. With a Milky Way in his hand, he was sure the room was still secure. His daily ritual was to waddle to a vending machine only thirty feet down the hall. What could have happened in the few minutes that he was away from Jeremy's door? Besides, he was off duty in thirty minutes and he couldn't wait to clock out.

While making his getaway, the phony doctor opened the door a few inches and saw the guard returning to his post. Wilson's eyes shot open when he noticed a green blur leaving the room.

"Hey, you! Wait!" Wilson demanded.

A man in green County Memorial scrubs darted down the hall and ducked sharply then bolted down the hall.

"Hold it right there!" Wilson repeated while raising a fist in the air.

The man ignored him, shoved a laundry cart out of his way, and forced himself into a crowded elevator. The others in the elevator looked at him strangely as he nervously pounded the "Lobby" button.

Wilson lumbered to catch up, but could only watch as the elevator doors closed. The perpetrator was already on his escape route through the main hospital lobby. Wilson turned to catch his breath. *Who was that doctor…and why did he run?* Wilson's heart pounded as he feared something had gone wrong and wondered what to do next. Hospital personnel had been coming and going all day long, and all of the hospital uniforms blended together.

Wilson snagged his radio and called the receptionist. "This is Officer Wilson…"

"Who?"

"The security guard…for Staymour's room! Stop the next doctor that leaves the elevator!"

"Stop a doctor? Why?" the woman repeated in confusion.

"Just listen to me…he's white, about five-eight, and wearing hospital scrubs. He's an imposter…and just ran out of Staymour's room!"

As the receptionist hung up with Wilson, the elevator doors opened, and the crowd of people dispersed slowly into the hospital lobby. The receptionist spotted a man weaving in and out of the crowd.

"Hey you, STOP RIGHT THERE!" she yelled.

He looked back for a second but then exited the hospital. Although security chased the culprit, he was way ahead of them. He sprinted down the alley and jumped into his car. The car peeled away, turned on Third Street, and was soon out of site.

7

LIZ CIRCLES BACK TO COUNTY MEMORIAL

Liz worried constantly about her brother. Her head pounded as she drove through the pouring rain toward her Springboro home. She speed-shifted the BMW and headed northbound on I-75. While driving, Liz argued with her conscience.

"He'll survive, Liz… stay positive," she mumbled.

"Positive?" her conscience fired back. *"How can I stay positive when my only brother is in a life-threatening coma?"*

A lone tear flowed down her cheek as she feared the worst. She was still awestruck over the whole incident. *Jay's in a coma…and nobody can tell me how long it will last! Days, weeks, months?*

At that moment there was a sad country song on the radio. The song's lyrics struck home when Liz heard them:

If I was only there to tell you…tell you that I'm here,
Only there to show you…show you that I care.

I love you like no other,
'cause I need you, you're my brother…

The lyrics echoed in Liz's head. She was approaching the Tylersville Road exit when her cell rang. Upon answering, she was surprised at what she heard. It was the hospital staff telling her that something terrible had happened to Jeremy.

"You've got to be kidding me…I'll be right there." She ended the call and slammed her palm on the steering wheel in disgust.

"Damn it! This is unbelievable. What could happen next?"

She swung the BMW to the berm and did an immediate U-turn through the muddy median. The sports car bounced and fishtailed twice before finally reaching Southbound I-75 toward Cincinnati. Even her beamer would take thirty minutes to get back downtown. Like a maniac, she zigzagged through the traffic and honked continuously at anyone who got in her way.

When she reached County Memorial, Liz swung into the closest parking spot and slammed on the brakes. She got out of her car and darted between parked vehicles leading to the hospital lobby. Her heart was pounding as she pushed the speed dial button on her cell. Finally, there was a voice.

"Hello?" Heath answered.

"Honey, get back to the hospital! Something has happened to Jeremy."

"I'll be right there," he shot back. She slid the phone back into her purse and stepped into the packed elevator. He would have to be on the fifth floor! The elevator doors opened and she walked quickly to Reception. She looked over the counter and saw Mrs. McNamara, who was counseling a patient's family.

"Excuse me," Liz interrupted abruptly. "You called me about Jeremy."

"Oh, Ms. Staymour. Thanks for returning so quickly." Mrs. McNamara excused herself from the other patient's family and pulled Liz aside. Her training didn't cover how to handle frustrated sisters of comatose patients. Mrs. McNamara noticed that onlookers in the waiting room were eavesdropping on the conversation.

"Here's a conference room," she said. They sat down at the table, and Mrs. McNamara continued her explanation.

"I'm embarrassed to tell you that there has been a breach at the hospital—an intruder snuck into your brother's room."

"You're kidding me! Who was it? What happened?" she demanded.

"An man disguised in hospital scrubs was seen leaving your brother's room."

"He wasn't a hospital employee? Then who was he?"

"The police are investigating."

"How did this happen? You people can't be this stupid! Tell me more..." Liz pleaded.

Mrs. McNamara apologized and continued. "The security guard stepped away for a minute and someone in scrubs snuck into your brother's room."

Liz peered angrily at Mrs. McNamara and felt like grabbing her by the throat. Noticing Liz's sudden reaction, Mrs. McNamara closed the conference room door, turned, and continued her explanation.

"The guard immediately alerted hospital security to be on the lookout for an imposter in hospital scrubs."

"And did they catch him?" Liz probed.

"Unfortunately," Mrs. McNamara continued, "when the elevator doors opened, there was mass hysteria, and people were scattering through the lobby. Our security staff spotted the man and immediately chased him down an alley—but somehow the man escaped."

"This is inexcusable," Liz shouted. She felt her face becoming flushed with anger. She took a moment to collect her thoughts and then finally spoke again in a normal tone.

"What happened to Jeremy? What happened in his room?" Liz demanded.

Mrs. McNamara paused and then continued. "After the intrusion, the staff closely examined Jeremy. A nurse noticed that some of Jeremy's medical equipment had been tampered with."

"You're kidding…what equipment? Is he okay?"

"His respirator and heart monitor were removed," Mrs. McNamara admitted in an embarrassed tone.

"NO!" Liz screamed. "This can't be!"

"The doctors are hoping he'll recover, but there's an outside chance he may need emergency surgery."

"No way! When can I talk to a doctor? It'd better be soon, or I'll be on the phone with my lawyers."

"In just a few moments, honey," Mrs. McNamara assured as she put her arm around Liz to comfort her. "Dr. Billings will explain everything when he completes the examination. They are watching Jeremy closely and will not leave his side until he is stabilized."

Liz was horrified at this strange turn of events. She wondered how this could have happened in a tightly guarded hospital room.

What in the world was Jeremy involved in? And who was trying so hard to kill him? Liz's head throbbed as she struggled to make sense of the situation.

———

Kinsey was driving when his cell buzzed.

"What's the word?"

"It's done," Kinsey bragged.

"Are you sure? Staymour's dead?"

"Well, not yet, but the entire hospital's in chaos. It'll take those yo-yos an eternity to find a serum—by then, it'll be too late," Kinsey gloated.

"What the hell did you give him--rat poison?" asked the gravelly voice of his superior in New York.

"No, but something just as potent…and he's probably straight-lining right now." Kinsey smiled as he admired his mastery. He looked in his rearview mirror to ensure that he wasn't being followed. He noticed that he was in the clear. Then he continued speaking to his superior.

"So, when do I get the money?" Kinsey asked in a cocky tone.

"When I see the obituary in the paper…and not a minute sooner." The man hung up and Kinsey did the same. He stared out the window at the passing trees along the road. He stayed on residential roads so he wouldn't arouse further suspicion.

8

HELP FROM SOUTH AFRICA

B ack at the hospital, the doctors and staff were stirring frantically around the bed of their comatose patient—and senior management was wondering how they would explain if Staymour died. How would they protect the hospital's interest? This form of negligence could be trouble…and probably a lawsuit.

How could that dumb-ass rent-a-cop allow someone to slip by him and get into Staymour's room? James Zachary wondered. The hospital president pondered the chain of events as he observed the recovery efforts from an observatory window high above the operating table.

Okay, Zach, what kind of lies can we conjure up this time? A negligence suit would cost millions and maybe my job. A total stranger dressed in scrubs sneaks into the hospital and enters the ICU room of a high-profile, comatose patient!

Doctors, nurses, and real interns continued examining Jeremy. They were perplexed when they saw him going into convulsions.

Each passing minute was critical—he was dying right in front of the doctors' eyes.

Nervous relatives were becoming unruly in the waiting room. Liz Staymour was the chief protester who was still firing tough questions at the reception staff.

"How can this happen in a secure hospital room? We're paying the hospital big bucks to care for my brother…and so far you've failed, Mrs. McNamara!"

"Ms. Staymour, I assure you—"

"You assure ME? I didn't make it a half-hour up the road before I had to turn around!"

Mrs. McNamara was wondering how long she could control her own temper now. *How long can I make up excuses?*

"Ms. Staymour…I apologize for what happened to your brother, but…" Heath appeared out of nowhere and wedged himself between them.

"Heath? I thought you were at work," she said in a softer voice.

"I was headed there, but now I'm here." She stared at him in a perplexed manner.

"Liz, honey…" Heath continued. "Let's just sit down a moment in the waiting room."

"But Heath…"

He covered her lips with a gentle palm before she could finish. Then, he wrapped his free arm around her affectionately and gently steered her toward the waiting room. When Liz's back was turned, Heath signaled apologetically to Mrs. McNamara.

Heath and Liz sat down for a few minutes to discuss the latest events. Each of them whispered silent prayers. They wondered if Jeremy would survive. And if so, could he somehow identify the perpetrator?

————

The doctors were examining the fluid in Staymour's IV bag. Since the IV fluid contained no foreign substances, the doctors and nurses re-examined every inch of their patient's body.

"Are there any injection marks on the patient?" Dr. Billings asked. The medical staff carefully examined Jeremy's entire body from head to toe with a magnifying glass. After ten minutes, Dr. Billings confirmed that there were none.

"He probably poured the drug into Mr. Staymour's IV," Dr. Billings yelled. Unfortunately, the IV stand was knocked over and the bag was missing.

With the clock ticking down, Dr. Billings ran a few desperate tests to identify the drug in Jeremy's bloodstream. The drug had to be diagnosed quickly. Then they ran a test for COVID-19 and it came up negative.

Three more tests and all came up negative. Would Jeremy's system be strong enough to avoid cardiac arrest? Dr. Billings sweated as the examination continued. Once the drug was identified, it would appear on the monitor. But the screen just flashed the words "Testing in progress."

There was no way to speed up the test. Two minutes passed and no results. Then the monitor lit up again. This time it flashed "Unknown Drug." As a last ditch effort, the medical team sent a message on the hospital's Poison Network of medical professionals across the world. The message described Jeremy's symptoms as the result of the intrusion. Hopefully, someone in the huge network could identify the drug and provide a serum.

Jeremy's symptoms worsened. He had convulsions and his organs were failing. Time was all he needed… just a little more time.

———

In a board room at an undisclosed location, LD discussed the options with his superiors. Seated at the head of the table was Jerome Bedford, the fifty-year-old ringleader of the corporation. The mission was known by a select few. Each of them was sworn to secrecy regarding their work. None of the worker bees dared to ask the name of the company. Instead, they were forced to perform tasks blindly while having a limited knowledge of the mission.

The meeting began with some small talk and soon afterward, there was a discussion about Jeremy Staymour. Kinsey decided that he would be the first to bring up the question that the others were also wondering. He stood and addressed the group.

"Why are we still trying to kill Staymour?" he began. "He won't sing now that he's in la-la land."

"I'm quite aware of that, but we can't risk it," LD responded. "The coma could last for days, months, or even years. We can't risk Staymour telling the cops what he knows. So who did you send in to finish the job?"

"It was me," Kinsey said. "That punk pissed me off when he backed out of the deal. He knows too much, so he's dangerous."

"You're right about that. Did you finish him off?"

"Yes, there's no way he could've survived," Kinsey answered quickly. "I poured a nice little cocktail into Staymour's IV."

"Are you sure he's dead this time?" LD insisted.

After a short pause, Kinsey spoke. "The hospital staff is probably tagging Staymour's big toe."

"Well let's not be overconfident," LD said, "not until we hear the news report that he's dead!"

LD glared at his subordinate. "Call me when you get confirmation."

"You'll be the first to know, sir" Kinsey replied. When LD adjourned the meeting, all of the men stood in unison. Stokely and the officers shook hands with LD and wished him good luck.

———

The medical team at County Memorial was scrambling as Staymour's condition worsened by the hour. A group of hospital specialists were in front of their laptops. They scrolled frantically for possible responses from hospital special research teams. They had to identify the chemical that was used. So far nothing.

Jeremy's biggest enemy was time. After an hour of no findings from any of the research centers, Jeremy's prognosis was very grim. His temperature rose to 103 degrees and his skin was reddening. The doctors and nurses were very worried and had no answers.

Ten more minutes passed and it seemed like ten hours. The County Memorial drug experts were still posting to various research centers across the world, but none of the teams came up with a solution or a possible serum. Jeremy's vitals were still worsening and the medical staff was preparing an excuse for Liz and the rest of the Staymour family.

Just when it appeared completely hopeless, there was a slight glimmer of hope. Halfway around the world, a South African doctor in a tiny trailer was reviewing Jeremy's blood charts from an internet posting. Aware that Jeremy's life was down to less than an hour, Dr. Maxa needed to work quickly.

"I'm so close!" he whispered. He continued reviewing the many pages of diagrams in his medical journal. In less than ten minutes, he spotted three potential matches. Seconds later he narrowed it to two and then a possible match!

While looking in the microscope, Dr. Maxa looked at the slide and then quickly shifted to diagrams in the medical journal he had open. Seconds later he jumped in the air. "There it is…I've got it!" he yelled. "The chemical is a toxic substance that is little known in the States. The cocktail of chemicals is known in Africa as LRG-A," he spoke into his voice recorder. "It is a very rare drug because of its strong side effects."

Next, Dr. Maxa perused other reliable sources to confirm his findings and to identify the proper serum. After twenty minutes of review, Dr. Maxa was confident that his findings were accurate. He grabbed his cell and contacted Jeremy's medical team.

"County Memorial…" the receptionist answered.

"Hello, this is Dr. Raju Maxa from the South African Research Center. May I talk to Dr. Billings please?"

"One moment, doctor," the receptionist said as she motioned to Billings. "It's a doctor from South Africa. Says he needs to talk to you immediately regarding patient Staymour."

Dr. Billings fumbled for his phone while still concentrating on his laptop. "This is Dr. Billings."

"Good afternoon, doctor. My name is Dr. Raju Maxa in Johannesburg."

Dr. Billings paused for a moment to process what he had just heard. A call from South Africa? He cleared his throat and then responded. "Thanks for calling, doctor," Billings began. "How can I help you?"

"Hello. Thanks for taking my call," he began. "I saw your posting on the Staymour case. I have been researching this in our most recent medical sites, and I believe I have a finding."

"You do?" Billings replied while rolling his eyes at the staff. "That's very encouraging," Billings said and then sipped his coffee. He had been through this drill about a dozen times—a renegade doctor, from some far away country, identifies a miracle serum and saves the world.

"Yes sir," Raju continued. "I have a finding and I'm confident that this one will work. You see," Dr. Maxa continued, "Mr. Staymour's symptoms and blood chart matched a finding."

"Yes, and what did you find?" Billings asked with great skepticism.

"I have determined that the intrusive chemical is most likely a toxin known as LRG-A," Dr. Maxa responded. Suddenly, Dr. Billing's curiosity was raised.

"LRG-A? What's that?"

"It's a little-known chemical in lawn fertilizer—it was originated by a scientist here in Africa. It's not meant for humans. If administered in concentrated doses, the chemical is lethal."

"Interesting, but can you confirm your findings through some other chemical experts?" Dr. Billings asked.

"Well…" Maxa replied in his strong South African accent. "I'm ninety-eight percent positive. I've already confirmed it in two journals." Noticing a stunned silence on the other end, the excited Dr. Maxa continued reporting details of his findings.

Dr. Billings started feeling some hope. His heart accelerated as he listened to the foreign doctor report the details. "LRG-A..." he repeated as he motioned to his assistant. The assistant then grabbed a medical journal and quickly thumbed through the pages. Within seconds, the assistant was nodding his head as he read about the chemical's effects.

"Thanks for your valuable research," Dr. Billings said as he wrapped up the call with Dr. Maxa. "We'll run a few pre-tests and see if we can confirm your findings. Hopefully, we can save Mr. Staymour."

Within thirty minutes, the poison staff quickly located a serum in Columbus. A medical chopper was already on its way for the twenty-five-minute flight to County Memorial. The doctors prayed that it was soon enough. Was there still time to save Jeremy? Liz, Heath, and the aunt and uncle formed a prayer chain in the waiting room.

The helicopter landed on the roof of the hospital. An intern met the chopper and sprinted to the elevator and soon arrived at Jeremy's room. Dr. Billings and company grabbed the serum and rushed to Staymour's bedside. They administered the serum just minutes before their famous patient would have experienced extreme perspiration, followed by convulsions, and then massive cardiac arrest. Within two hours, all of his vitals were upgraded to normal. Somehow, Jeremy Staymour had dodged another attempt on his life!

———

When the corporation received the bad news about Staymour's miracle recovery, LD and the officers were livid. "Call an emergency meeting!" he lashed out at his people. "We need to come up with a new position on Staymour!"

(9)

A BAD CAR RIDE FOR LIZ

The two o'clock meeting went on as scheduled. LD, a very burly man, was at the head of the large oval table. The other attendees were Kinsey, Stokely, and Granger.

"As all of you know by now," LD began, "our friend, Mr. Staymour, is still alive." Kinsey lowered his head in shame and hoped that nothing more would be said about his botched attempt on Staymour's life.

"The news programs have reported that all new JTST company client accounts are on hold pending a complete investigation of Staymour's suspicious activities," LD said. He paused a moment and gazed at the others for emphasis. "So we're switching to a new plan." He flipped through slides as he spoke.

"After much thought, we've decided to ignore Jeremy Staymour for now," LD announced. "We're not sure if he'll ever wake up anyway."

"We're going to let him live?" Stokely asked.

"Yes. We've got connections with two doctors who will soon be transferred to County Memorial," LD bragged. "The two insiders will report to us on Staymour's health updates."

LD paused for a few seconds and studied the room. "Is the plan clear, gentlemen?"

Some small talk amongst the group followed a few closing comments. After adjourning the meeting, LD motioned to Kinsey.

"Kinsey, can I see you a moment?"

Stokely and the others adjourned and LD closed the door behind them. Kinsey's heart thumped wildly in anticipation. LD roughed up select partners in the corporation whenever they failed a mission.

LD paced slowly around the curve of the table and Kinsey waited in dread. A few more slow and calculated steps. Soon, LD stood directly behind Kinsey, who was still seated. LD rested his large hands on his frightful victim's shoulders. The massaging began. First mild pressure to the neck and shoulders. Then LD's fat fingers dug unmercifully into Kinsey's shoulder, causing him to squirm in pain.

"Ahhh!"

"You let me down, Kinz…can I trust you to continue the operation?" Kinsey squirmed some more. LD considered finishing Kinsey off with a lethal chokehold but he thought better of it. Not just yet.

LD dug his fingers into Kinsey's shoulders and continued the interrogation. "Can we still count on you, Mr. Kinsey?" LD repeated.

Kinsey squirmed in pain but couldn't say anything. Seconds later, he anguished but gathered enough energy to respond. "Yes, sir," he responded as his shoulder throbbed. First, a sharp burning in his neck, then it streamed to his shoulders and right arm.

"I thought so," LD replied. "I wasn't so kind to our men in the drive-by…they've conveniently disappeared. You don't want that to happen to you, do you?"

"No sir," Kinsey answered. "You can still count on me, sir! I swear!"

"I thought so…you're one of my best men." LD paused again before dropping the big one on Kinsey.

"There's something you can do to redeem yourself."

"What is it? I'll do whatever you want," Kinsey answered, his shoulder throbbing.

"With the new plan, we need you to kill Staymour's sister, Liz."

Kinsey acknowledged and then attempted to stand but LD shoved him back in his chair. The angry man squeezed Kinsey's shoulder for a third time causing him to bellow in pain. Make it stop!!

Seconds later, LD continued his explanation. "Our little friend, Ms. Staymour, has been snooping around and getting too close to the operation. She's been prying into Jeremy's business dealings—if left unchecked, we're afraid she'll discover who we are."

LD again paused for a few seconds. Then the old man bent down and looked eye-to-eye with Kinsey. "Do you understand what I am saying? Liz Staymour MUST be eliminated…"

Kinsey had killed several people. He was paid handsomely each time and had little remorse. But he had never killed a woman and that bothered him.

"It's not murder, Kinsey—just arrange a little accident…she'll never know what happened," LD mumbled. He puffed on his cigar and cracked an evil smile. Smoke rings floated to the ceiling.

Kinsey was released and walked slowly down the long corridor to the exit. He hated his dreadful life. His shoulders had bruising imprints from LD's monster grip. He was trapped within the corporation's mission. How could he kill a woman, especially Liz Staymour?

Kinsey drove his car for three or four miles with no particular destination. Suddenly, a traffic light turned red and he jammed on the brakes, nearly T-boning another car. He pulled away and turned onto a residential street. He parked the car and then slammed his palm on the steering wheel.

His blood boiling, Kinsey realized that he had to obey LD and his evil ways. He turned the car around in a driveway and returned to the main road. A few minutes later, he saw a billboard that read "Earn extra cash…today."

Kinsey smiled and reverted to his criminal self. He dreamed of the huge payoff—soon he would be surrounded by piles of cold cash.

"I'll make millions. The big bucks will come when I get rid of Liz Staymour. Carry out the mission," he reminded himself. "Carry out the mission."

The sign ahead said "Springboro, 10 miles."

———

Five hours after Liz fell asleep, an intruder wandered outside her home. A man in a dark hooded sweatshirt peered into her car with a small flashlight. Liz had left her car in the driveway that evening because they were storing a furniture delivery in the garage.

The man peered both ways before crossing the street toward Liz's car. He jimmied the driver's side door lock. Once seated in the car, he yanked the hood release, which made a popping sound. In the dead of night, the noise was louder than expected. He looked up nervously at the curtains, but they were still.

He walked to the front of the car, raised the hood, and quickly surveyed the engine. He could sabotage the master cylinder to make the brakes fail.

After following Liz to work one day, Kinsey knew that she had to drive down a steep, winding hill. If he calculated correctly, the brake cylinder would empty near a dangerous curve. If that happened, the brakes would fail near any of the three embankments. If the brake fluid drained too quickly, Liz would realize it in time and pull over to the side of the road and call for help.

After some careful thought, the man crawled under the car. He left the master cylinder intact and cut the brake lines instead. He spotted the main line and made a thin slice. Brake fluid dripped slowly from the line.

Kinsey hoped Liz wouldn't spot brake fluid when she backed out of her driveway. He prayed that she wouldn't suspect problems with her car on the drive to work. If she noticed car trouble, that would foil the entire plan.

The scenario was simple—her car loses its brakes at the precise moment down the winding road. A serious crash would ensue.

The scheme had to work. LD wouldn't permit another slipup.

———

At five thirty, Heath and Liz stirred to the sound of her alarm. She laid there for a minute or two, and then headed to the shower. Ten minutes later, Liz quickly brushed her teeth and headed down the hall toward the coffee pot.

"Morning, honey," Liz said.

Heath was groggy but managed a half smile. "Man, I need a cup of coffee."

———

Kinsey sat in his car across the street. Just sat and waited. At 5:50, he peered upward at the second-floor window and saw a shadowy figure through the curtains. He assumed the figure was Liz returning to the bedroom.

Kinsey smiled. The brake system was dripping nicely, so the evil plan was a go. He envisioned Liz's fateful drive to work. She would slam the brake pedal…down, up, down, up while screaming for her life. He calculated that her car would accelerate to over sixty down the steep and winding hill. He was confident that she would lose control with the sharp turns and narrow shoulder.

———

Liz hopped into her car and gathered her thoughts about work. She would be making a presentation in the afternoon. She checked her lipstick in her mirror and then backed out slowly. Not noticing the small puddle on the driveway, she waved at a neighbor who was also leaving for work. Then she threw the Beemer into first gear and headed out.

Minutes into her trip, she had a strange feeling that something wasn't quite right. Liz squirmed and struggled to get comfortable. Strangely, she heard a familiar male voice in her ear but she couldn't place it…She shook her head in an attempt to make the voice go away, but the eeriness continued…

Stop the car…something terrible is going to happen to you! Her mind screamed in alarm.

Liz slowed nearly to a stop but then continued driving. She was frightened at the familiar-sounding voice in her head. She adjusted her lap belt and struggled to get comfortable. "Where do I know that voice?" While driving past some small shops, she tested the brake pedal which felt a little squishy, but she wasn't alarmed. Ten seconds later she heard the voice again.

Liz, listen to me and pull over.

Now a strange feeling came over her. This time she recognized the voice. It was Jeremy and he was trying to warn her.

"This is nuts," Liz told herself. "Jeremy's in a coma…he's lying peacefully in his hospital bed…I'm not hearing his voice. Am I losing it?" She planned on calling the doctor when she got to work. She concluded that she was just under too much stress lately.

Liz shook her head and ignored the warnings. She turned onto a steep and winding two-lane road called Crane's Run. The car maneuvered around a sharp bend and started down the steep hill.

The road curved sharply to the left, causing Liz to panic. She jammed on the brake pedal and this time it went all the way to the floor! She tested the pedal again and it seemed to return to normal. She shrugged it off as paranoia. The pads and rotors were just replaced. There was no reason for a silly thought like *the brakes may fail.*

The BMW continued down the curvy road. Liz glanced over the guardrail at the eighty-foot embankment to the brush below. She again tapped the brake pedal and it seemed normal. But when she depressed it a third time, the pedal went to the floor again.

"What the hell's going on?" she yelled. When the car did not slow down, Liz yanked the wheel left and narrowly missed a guard rail. She suddenly feared for her life.

The car continued to accelerate and began to swerve. A nervous Liz switched to panic mode. The Beemer clipped one guard rail and then bounced off of another. The car fishtailed and Liz's head slammed violently against the driver's window. She reached for the emergency brake lever, but it also failed.

"Stop! Why won't it stop?" she screamed as she continued stomping on the limp brake pedal. Now Liz was desperate.

The car scraped another guard rail before going airborne over a small embankment. When it landed, the dented car bounced three or four times, spun completely around, and crashed abruptly into a tree.

Liz must have blacked out for the first few minutes after impact. When she awoke, the first thing she noticed was the car's hood which was bent slightly upward. She heard the radiator hissing. When she was finally able to focus, she saw steam rising around the dented hood. Liz's head was resting on the side airbag, which resembled a giant pillow. She was still breathing, but barely. And she had a deep cut on her right cheek.

"Uhhhh," Liz grunted. She felt a sharp pain in her right side, which made breathing difficult. *"Liz, are you okay?"* The imaginary voice shouted in a return appearance.

Still in a fog, Liz sat in the wreckage for a few more seconds in stunned silence. She wanted to answer, but couldn't mouth a word. She urgently fought to maintain consciousness.

Minutes later, Liz's eyelids became heavy and her vision faded in and out. Several cars passed on the road above, but no one noticed the crumpled vehicle in the wooded ravine below.

———

Several minutes later, the driver of a dark SUV noticed a dented guardrail and pulled over for a better look. A car door slammed and Kinsey ran over to the edge of the embankment. His eyes widened when he spotted Liz's smoldering car down below. He walked closer and focused on the dented license plate. He smiled when he saw the plate number—643CVL48—the number Kinsey had etched in his memory. Without hesitation and according to plan, he pulled out his cell.

"It's her...and I think she's dead. She's gotta be!" There was a pause and then he continued, "Okay...I'll make sure."

He ended the call and then stepped carefully down the muddy slope. When he made it to the car and looked inside, he wasn't so sure that Liz was dead. He knew that he had to work quickly or the steaming car could ignite and kill both of them.

"She has blood all over her face and arms," he reported on his cell. Then Kinsey slipped the phone back in his pocket and tugged repeatedly on the driver's door. Nothing. It wouldn't budge. So he ran to the passenger's side and yanked abruptly on that handle. More steam and whistling louder.

"Come on…come on!" he screamed as he yanked harder on the handle. Finally, the door creaked loudly and opened about six inches. He pulled again and it opened about the width of his body. He wedged himself through the opening and sat on the passenger seat.

The driver resembled the woman in the picture, although her face was scratched and bloodied. He searched for Liz's wrist but it was wedged under the airbag. He placed two fingers on her neck. A faint pulse, and she was barely breathing. Unsure what to do next, Kinsey grabbed his cell and made one last call.

"I'm still here with Staymour's sister…" He hesitated for a second when he heard an approaching siren.

"Are those sirens?"

"Yes sir," Kinsey replied worriedly.

"Is she still alive?"

"Yes, but barely."

"Put a cap in her and get out of there."

Kinsey pulled out his pistol, but in his haste, the silencer fell to the floor of the car.

Since the emergency workers were getting close, there was no time to shoot her since the noise of the gun would be his demise. Kinsey wiggled out of the wrecked car, ran up the hill to his vehicle, and fled the scene. He escaped just before the ambulance arrived.

Five emergency team workers ran down the hill. Could they save Liz's life?

10

THE FLING AND THE SPREE

Ricki Valentes was aboard a flight to Bloomington, Minnesota. Time to get away and spend some serious money. Girl time without Daniel. An urgent shopping spree for the latest multimillionaire.

She walked down the aisle of the plane and shoved her bags in the overhead. She scooted across to the window seat and silenced her phone.

As passengers made their way down the aisle, Ricki pulled out a travel magazine from the seat pouch in front of her. She browsed through an advertisement about a cruise vacation. She perused a few more pages and then looked up.

A handsome man in his thirties pulled out his boarding pass and checked his seat number. He smiled at the seated woman and secured his bag overhead. As the tall man lowered his athletic frame into the seat, Ricki's mind played tricks on her. She imagined a set of defined abs under his shirt.

The man buckled his seatbelt and got situated in his seat. Ricki wanted to say something but no words came out of her mouth. She directed her attention to her magazine and pretended to read. After a few awkward seconds of silence, the man spoke first.

"Hi there," he said with a smile.

Ricki's heart pounded, and she felt a warmth coming over her. She wiggled nervously in her seat before responding.

"Hello…" Ricki said with a slight squeak in her voice. The man glanced at his cell and scanned his text messages.

Ricki was already in a slap-happy mood and now a rather attractive man was sitting next to her. A minute or two passed in silence. Finally, Ricki decided to break the ice.

"I'm Ricki," she said while offering her hand.

"Hi, Kent, nice to meet you." When the man offered his hand, Ricki wished the hand shake could have lasted longer. His hands were large and warm.

"On a business trip?" Ricki asked.

"Oh…yes…I've got a meeting in Minneapolis. I missed my connection and grabbed this one. Need to be there by two-thirty."

Ricki looked at her watch and chuckled. "That will be tough since this plane won't arrive until two."

"Yeah, I guess they'll get over it." Kent smiled. "It's a good thing I own the company."

Ricki raised an eyebrow and grinned. The flight attendants were demonstrating the seat belts and the emergency breathing apparatus.

"I get so tired of all this pre-flight stuff," Kent complained to Ricki.

"Yeah, I think we could figure out how to use the masks, don't you?"

Kent answered in a way that was playful and flirty. Then the pilot came on the intercom and asked the flight attendants to secure the cabin for departure. Ricki felt somewhat guilty for flirting, especially since she was involved with Daniel. But now she had a sudden boldness about her. After all, she was a multi-millionaire… she deserved a little mischief.

She glanced over at Kent and liked what she saw. She tried not to stare and she hoped that she wouldn't stumble all over her words. *Wow!* she thought as she turned the oxygen knob in the panel above. Five minutes later, the plane was still climbing to its cruising altitude. Kent pulled out an investment magazine. Ricki wanted to keep the conversation moving.

She didn't want to seem annoying and she didn't want to pry. Then the guilt hit her again. *What am I doing? I've got Daniel…and I'm in love with him.* Ricki finally regained her composure and told herself to stop flirting. She flipped through a few more pages of her magazine. The flight attendant rolled the refreshment cart next to Kent when the plane leveled off.

"What would you like, sir?"

"I'll have a seven-seven, please."

"And you, ma'am?'

"Uh…just a Coke."

The flight attendant poured both drinks and passed them to Kent and Ricki. In the minutes that followed, Kent did not read much of his magazine. Instead, he shared some small talk with Ricki. He learned that she was unmarried and enjoyed football games. They had an interesting conversation during the flight and they seemed to enjoy one another's company.

As the plane made its initial approach to Minneapolis, Kent whispered something in Ricki's ear. She smiled and nodded her head. Soon the plane landed and the passengers gathered their bags. Against her better judgment, Ricki had a crush on this guy. She couldn't seem to refrain.

Kent and Ricki exited the plane and headed through the terminal. As they were walking, Kent pulled out his cell and sent a text to his business partner. Then he buried the cell and re-engaged in conversation with Ricki.

"They weren't too happy that my plane arrived a little late," he said.

"Did they start the meeting without you?" Ricki asked with a smirk.

"Sure did. I guess I'm not as important as I thought." Upon reaching baggage claim, Kent and Ricki watched the endless stream of luggage. Ricki's bag arrived first, and she grabbed it. Kent spotted his bag a few seconds later.

Enjoying each other's company, they headed toward ground transportation. Kent slowed down a step and gently pulled Ricki aside.

"Ricki…there's something I need to ask you," he said. While at first looking downward, he slowly raised his eyes until they met hers.

"Can I call you during your stay? Maybe get a cup of coffee?" he asked softly, but confidently.

Ricki's heart seemed to skip a beat and she was totally unprepared to answer. She looked up at the six-footer and admired his dimpled smile. His dark eyes were strong and vibrant. She hesitated and didn't immediately answer. She took a few more steps toward her taxi and Kent followed her.

"I'd really like to see you again," he said.

There were a few moments of silence as they continued to walk. Finally, she turned and smiled. "Well, I suppose," she giggled. Ricki got out a small piece of paper from her purse and jotted down her hotel phone number.

Kent folded the note and slipped it in his pocket. He smiled and waved to Ricki as she hopped into a taxi.

111

GUILTY FEELINGS AND THE TRIP HOME

D aniel Flarity was concerned when he couldn't reach Ricki on her cell. The text message read "No Service."

"Where in the hell is she?" he muttered angrily while shifting gears. Three rings, four rings…and voicemail. His mind wandered as he pulled off the exit ramp toward her neighborhood. He tried to clear his mind, but he couldn't. He continued driving and envisioned the scenarios. Was she in an accident? Dammit, why won't she answer?

He drove up Cobblegate and swung into the driveway. As he ran to the door, Daniel prayed that he wouldn't find her dead on her living room floor. He pulled the keys from his pocket and clumsily dropped them on the porch. He cussed again as he opened the door.

"Ricki?" he yelled as he entered the home. No response. Then he yelled up the stairs. "Ricki…are you home?" Still nothing. Nervously, he ran through the living room to the kitchen. Turning toward the counter, he spotted a note lying by the phone. He picked it up and began reading.

> *Honey, please don't be mad but I booked a flight for the weekend. Going shopping to spend some of the lottery money. Just a little getaway…Don't worry…I'll be back Monday.*
>
> *I love you!*
>
> *-Ricki*

The note seemed innocent, but Daniel feared that there was more to the story. For a few seconds, he just stared aimlessly around the room. Then he folded the note into quarters and clenched it tightly in his fist.

"Damn her!" he shouted aloud. He continued pacing as he searched for answers. First he was worried about Ricki's safety…and then his selfish thoughts took over. *What if she dumps me and takes off with all the money and never returns? The way my investments are falling, I'd probably have to go back to work!*

In anger, he threw the crumpled note on the table. He looked nervously at his watch which read ten-thirty. *I just can't believe it.* He feared that something may have happened to her. Should he report that she is missing?

He shook his head and staggered to the refrigerator. He popped open a beer. He chugged half of it and sat at the table. He paused a few seconds to gather his thoughts and then un-crumpled the note and re-read it.

He got through the first sentence and then took another drink of beer. *Why did she need some time away? We're in love.* Then he read on. *Was it an out-of-town shopping trip? That's not like Ricki. She wouldn't just take off like that. She's gotta work on Monday. Although, she doesn't need money anymore.*

He chugged the last few swallows then checked his voicemail— no messages. His mind searched for answers but he had none. After drinking two more beers, he pounded his fist on the wall. Then he rubbed is head and walked away. *I'm sure it's nothing…she's probably playing some kind of joke on me.*

Daniel sighed and walked slowly to the living room. He sat down on the recliner, grabbed the remote, and flipped through the channels. Finally, he clicked on a Business channel. He watched the ticker, but he wasn't reading it—he was too distraught over Ricki. Then a few seconds later, something on the ticker caught his eye.

JTST trades are on hold pending the Federal investigation…CEO remains in a coma.

Daniel shook his head and had a worried look in his eyes. *My girlfriend's money is tied up and now she's gone. She's not shopping—that's just an excuse.* He paced into the kitchen. He sat at the table and buried his head in his palms. *I still think I should report her disappearance. I don't care about the shopping, but where in the hell is she? I wouldn't even know where to look!*

After another hour of brainstorming, Daniel couldn't wait any longer. Ricki's whereabouts were killing him. He pounded his fist on the wall as he contemplated what to do. Head pounding, he threw an empty beer can at the wall. He paced from the kitchen to the living room, where he found the sofa. Ten minutes later, he conked out for a couple of hours.

He dreamt of driving a jaguar down a tree-lined country road. Then the dream continued.

> *The car moved slowly, and the chrome spokes flickered. In the dream, Daniel slowed the car to a stop. He flipped the car door open and sprinted toward the huge country porch where Ricki stood. She was wearing a white halter top and jeans shorts. She was smiling at him and motioning for him to climb the steps and join her on the huge wooden porch. She continued motioning for him to join her. Two steps, three steps. He continued climbing the porch steps toward his millionaire girlfriend. She remained smiling and she motioned again.*
>
> *When Daniel reached the final step, he felt a strong resistance. He saw her bright silhouette slowly fading, and fading, getting fainter and fainter until the entire silhouette completely disappeared. "Ricki!" Daniel yelled with outstretched arms.*

As his eyes followed the fading light, he was awakened by a screeching noise. He popped out of the recliner in alarm. His heart pounding and sweat dripping from his brow, he staggered slowly, shook his head groggily, and tried to focus.

He discovered that the loud noise was not part of his dream, but the screech of airbrakes from the garbage truck on the street. Realizing that it was only a dream, Daniel breathed a sigh of relief.

However, his concerns about real-life Ricki quickly resurfaced. She was gone, and something didn't feel right.

———

Ricki and Kent walked through a Minneapolis shopping mall. They visited some specialty stores and Ricki settled on an amazing Louis Vuitton purse. She pulled out her MasterCard and slid it through the card reader. She smiled as she enjoyed the shopping spree.

Kent stood behind Ricki and tickled her ribs while she was finalizing the purchase. Ricki squirmed a little and smiled at him.

"Stop it, Kent," she said, although she secretly enjoyed it. The cashier handed Ricki the luxury purse and receipt, then the couple turned to leave the store.

As they walked away, Ricki realized that this new acquaintance had gone too far. *What am I doing? I love Daniel and yet I'm shopping in a strange city with someone that I just met on the flight.*

They continued walking through the crowded mall. As Ricki looked around, other couples were walking by and some of them were holding hands. As she continued reflecting, Ricki had tremendous guilt feelings. She was embarrassed about the fling. Her intention was merely to skip town, go shopping, and return home.

Kent was babbling on about his college days and the pranks he pulled at rush parties. Ricki only heard about three or four words of the story because her mind was still on Daniel. *I can't do this. I need to ditch this guy and get out of here!*

As they walked further down the mall, Ricki thought of a plan. "Hey Kent," she interrupted while her brown eyes glanced upward.

"Yeah?" he replied and smiled.

"I'm going in here to look for a pair of jeans and a blouse. Why don't you go to the sports store and shop for some guy stuff? I'll meet you back here in about fifteen or twenty," Ricki said flirtatiously.

"Sounds good…see you in about fifteen," Kent answered.

Ricki walked to the entrance of the clothing store then turned to ensure Kent was out of sight. She darted past the specialty stores, sprinted down a series of escalators, and left the mall.

Ricki glanced to her left and noticed that a transit bus was beginning to edge forward. She waved her arms and signaled for the bus to pull over. She was relieved that the driver saw her and stopped for one more passenger. Ricki hopped onto the bus and stuffed a couple of dollars in the money acceptor. Once seated, she tapped Daniel's number on her cell and waited anxiously for the ringtones.

"Hello?"

"Daniel…it's me."

"Where in the hell are you?" he shouted into the phone. "I've been worried sick about you!"

"I'm actually in Minneapolis, Danny." There was a long pause on the other end of the phone. "You're not going to believe this, but I went on a shopping spree, just enjoying some of the windfall."

Daniel was speechless. "What is wrong with you, Ricki? Have you completely lost your mind? And why would you sneak away to an out-of-town mall, and why Minnesota?"

Ricki wiped some tears from her eyes, but then collected her thoughts before speaking. "Well, I don't know what came over me. The thought of all the money…it was making me crazy. I didn't plan anything…I just jumped on a plane for the thrill of it! I'm sorry, honey!"

Daniel probably felt betrayed but he said nothing. There would be time later. Ricki, on the other hand, wasn't about to spill her guts about her unexpected affair, so there was silence. After the awkward pause, they both spoke at the same time. Ricki politely continued— "shhhhh," she whispered into the phone. "Please don't worry. I'll hop the first plane out of here…I promise."

She whispered her goodbyes and quickly ended the call. A tear ran down her cheek as she was overridden with guilt. She looked out the window of the bus and stared at the passing trees. Ten minutes later, she stepped off the bus and waved down a taxi.

"Where will it be, ma'am?"

"Airport, please."

Upon her return to the Queen City, Ricki rushed in the front door and met Daniel. They hugged and kissed for a moment but the feelings were very awkward. Ricki apologized profusely and Daniel mostly stared at the ground. He was hurt and confused.

Ricki felt terrible about betraying him. After some careful wordsmithing, she got through the apology. "What was the best part of the trip?" Daniel finally mumbled.

"Lots of shopping in a very nice mall," she lied. Not a word was spoken about her little "fling" with Kent. Ricki prayed that her dark little secret would never rise to the surface.

12

RICKI MEETS LIZ

Liz was in County Memorial for seven days following her car accident over the small embankment. The police investigated the accident and had no had no idea who had cut her brake lines. Detective Lankford's team found the silencer on the floor of the passenger side and scrubbed it for prints. So far, there were no matches. The team was very perplexed as to why an unexplained silencer showed up in Liz's car at all. Very strange.

Liz was still sore from the accident, but was very lucky. She had no broken bones so she was cleared for release.

While the hospital was processing the discharge papers, Liz tried to process the latest events. Her life was in complete disarray. It wasn't enough that her brother was shot, landing him in a life-threatening coma, and then someone tried to poison him in his hospital bed! When they failed to kill Jeremy, someone sabotaged Liz's car, causing her brakes to fail mysteriously on a winding road.

Liz was getting a migraine as her thoughts continued. *This is like a horror movie! All this bad luck! I WILL get to the bottom of this. They'll have to put a bullet in my head to stop me!*

"You take care, Ms. Staymour…and good luck," Mrs. McNamara said at the reception desk.

"Thanks for your kind words," Liz replied as she forced a smile. "I'll be back in a few days to visit Jeremy."

"Okay, it was a pleasure caring for you. Nurse Curtis will wheel you to the front lobby."

Seconds later, an attractive nurse came around the corner and greeted Liz. "Hello, Ms. Staymour. I'm Angie Curtis." Liz looked at her curiously.

"You look familiar. Have we met?" Liz asked.

"I was a substitute nurse for your brother last week. I saw you when I was leaving his room."

"Oh, that's right. I forgot. There have been so many doctors and nurses around Jay the last month or so."

"I know, honey" Angie replied. "The entire staff is praying for your brother."

"I appreciate that," Liz replied.

"Well, hop in the wheelchair so we can get you out of here."

"I don't need it…I can walk to the lobby on my own," Liz answered.

"I'm sorry, hospital rules for all patients leaving this place."

Liz shrugged her shoulders but didn't argue. She slid into the wheelchair and Angie began rolling her down the hall.

As the elevator door was opening, Liz thought of a question that had been on her mind. "Angie, I don't know much about comas or how they work. Have you had much experience with comatose patients?"

"Well, I've been working here for about five years and your brother is about the fourth coma patient I've witnessed."

"How did the other three patients fare?"

As the elevator door closed, Angie continued. "There was a ten-year-old boy who was attacked by a vicious dog. Lost so much blood that he went into a coma."

"How long did his coma last? Did he ever snap out of it?"

"Lasted two or three months. Many of us on the staff wondered if he would ever awaken. Then one day while his mom was holding his hand and talking to him, he just opened his eyes."

"You're kidding!"

"Nope, and it nearly gave his mom a heart attack. Within minutes, he was able to turn his head slightly and make sounds."

"So did he recover?" Liz asked.

"Well, he's still going through therapy but the doctors expect a full recovery."

The elevator doors opened and Angie pushed Liz's wheelchair toward the front reception area.

"That's encouraging," Liz commented. "I hope my brother awakens soon. This is starting to wear on me." Liz paused a moment and then continued her probe. "What about the other two coma patients?"

"Oh yeah," Angie continued. "An eighty-year-old man fell down the stairs and struck his head violently, causing him to go into a coma. He ended up dying three days later."

"And the third one?" Liz asked.

"Oh, she was a woman in her thirties who was stabbed during a robbery in her home."

"Nice neighborhood," Liz said while rolling her eyes.

"Yeah…she was from Vine Street. That area is getting so bad that even the police are afraid to drive through there."

"So what happened to her?"

"She's been in a coma for five years. She seems to respond occasionally when people talk to her. One relative told the woman a joke and he swears the woman's cheek moved. The doctors think that she may have been trying to smile."

"It seems like there have been some miraculous stories over the years regarding coma patients," Liz mentioned while looking up at Angie. "I just hope Jay turns out to be one of those miracles."

"Me, too," Angie replied as she glanced outside and saw the taxi approaching.

"Well there's my ride," Liz said as the car approached. Angie angled the wheelchair near the door and helped Liz into the car.

"Take care now, Ms. Staymour."

"Thank you very much," Liz replied. She stepped out and the taxi drove away. Across the street, a late-model black Mustang pulled out and followed the taxi. The driver of the car was wearing dark sunglasses. It was Ricki Valentes.

———

As Liz walked slowly up her driveway, she noticed an approaching woman.

"Excuse me…Ms. Staymour?"

Liz stopped and stared blankly at the woman. "Yes, can I help you?"

"Hello, Ms. Staymour," the woman repeated as she offered her right hand. Liz obliged with a shallow handshake. "You may not know me. My name is Ricki Valentes."

Liz looked at Ricki strangely. She didn't recognize the lottery winner that recently grabbed headlines in the local news and all over the internet.

"Let me start by saying that I'm a lottery winner and I just invested the majority of the winnings in JTST, your brother's company."

"Wow, that's incredible," Liz said in amazement. "Congrats on the windfall!"

"Well thank you very much," Ricki said. "And you probably know JTST is not accepting new clients until more is known about your brother's coma and his general health conditions. Therefore, my account at JTST is in pending status."

"Oh okay. Hopefully, it won't be long," Liz said.

"Yes, hopefully. But the real reason that I'm here is to discuss my boyfriend's business dealings with your brother and his company," Ricki said.

Still intrigued about meeting a lottery winner, Liz asked Ricki to continue.

"Well, my boyfriend is an investor and I think he may be one of your brother's clients as well."

"He is?" Liz asked. "Is there some problem with that?"

"I'm not sure, but do you have a few moments to talk?"

"Sure…" Liz conceded. "Why don't you come in and we'll discuss this over a cup of coffee."

Liz normally would not invite a stranger into her house, but the way her week was going, she welcomed the company. She showed Ricki into the house and closed the door behind them. Neither woman noticed that a man with binoculars was sitting in a black Suburban behind Ricki's car.

"Have a seat at the table," Liz said as she motioned to the kitchen. Ricki pulled out a chair and slowly sat down. Liz headed to the counter and started a pot of gourmet coffee.

————

LD's goon waited out front for about an hour and nearly fell asleep. He was about to call in for further instructions when he noticed some activity. Liz's door opened and both of them were suddenly leaving.

While engaged in active discussion, the women hopped into Liz's new Lexus and sped off. The man in the Suburban tried to pull out but had to wait because of some sudden traffic. By the time he was able to pull out, the man lost sight of Liz's car.

"Damn it. I lost them!" he reported on his cell. The voice at the other end was really upset.

"Find them! And I mean NOW!"

"I'm on it, Boss!" the goon replied.

The Suburban accelerated and jockeyed wildly through the heavy traffic. The goon blew through a red light, nearly broadsided another vehicle, and hoped to catch Liz.

13

A SURPRISE VISIT TO JTST

Liz and Ricki were en route to Jeremy's office in Cincinnati. They had managed to lose LD's goon in traffic. Actually, they had no idea that he was behind them. They wanted to visit JTST and learn firsthand about Jeremy's business dealings.

"I can't believe you won the frickin' lottery," Liz commented. "How does it feel to be a multi-millionaire?"

Ricki smiled and shrugged her shoulders. "It's just surreal! Sometimes I have to pinch myself to make sure I'm not dreaming this whole thing."

"You're so lucky," Liz said.

"It was only this time...I've never won anything else in my life."

There was a short pause, then Liz continued. "So how much did you end up clearing after taxes?"

"Thirty-nine million."

Liz looked over at Ricki in awe. Then she quickly returned her eyes to the road. Luckily, she maneuvered around a large cardboard box in the highway.

Hardly affected by the near mishap, Liz was still intrigued by Ricki's giant windfall. "Wow," she said. "I'm happy for you and your good fortune."

"Well, thanks. It's been mostly good but there are a lot of vultures out there."

"Oh, I bet!"

"Yeah. Everyone is trying to sell me something or re-kindle a relationship with me."

"Ha, I bet! Well good luck keeping the wolves away," Liz said as she sped up to switch lanes. Neither of them spoke for a mile or two. Then Liz broke the silence.

"So how long has Daniel been investing with Jeremy's firm?" Liz asked as they drove past the Middletown exit. She had to slow down because there were so many orange barrels through the local road construction.

"Well I've known him for two and a half years and he's been in all kinds of investment opportunities since then. First it was real estate where he bought and rented some ranch-style homes. He started out small and worked his way up to his fifteenth property."

"Really? Sounds like he's had some good breaks over the years."

"Yeah, but he's told me it wasn't always easy for him," Ricki answered. "When he was a college student he was lucky to rub two nickels together. At one point it was a steady diet of peanut butter sandwiches."

Liz laughed before continuing. "So did he invest in anything other than real estate?"

"Well, four or five years ago, he jumped into mutual funds. I really couldn't tell you much more than that," Ricki said. Then she turned to Liz.

"What about your brother? How'd he grow his business so quickly? I thought that normally took years!"

"Well, I really haven't asked him…he's kind of private with his own investments, and even more so with his business dealings," Liz replied. "Sounds like both guys are really into investing."

"Yeah, Daniel's always reading investment books and watching investment videos online. I'm glad he's making money, but sometimes I think he's obsessed with it."

"Really? Why do you say that?" Liz asked.

"He can't stay focused on one thing. It's like, I love him to death, but sometimes he's kind of weird."

"How's that?" Liz asked.

"Well, we were relaxing on the couch the other day…"

"Just relaxing?" Liz jabbed.

"Yeah," Ricki said. "We were, well… watching a movie and he pulled away from me."

"Seems strange."

"Yeah, he just sat up quickly! For some reason, he was glued to an investment commercial. Mesmerized."

"That is weird," Liz said.

"Yeah, definitely strange behavior!"

There was a pause in the conversation, then Ricki continued. "Daniel's a great guy and we have a great relationship. But sometimes he gets geeky with his investment portfolio."

Liz listened intently to Ricki. "Did he have dealings with my brother?" she repeated.

"I've heard him mention Jeremy on his cell a few times. I think they even go to the same gym."

"Really?" Liz said. "I've never heard Jeremy mention his name."

Liz pulled the Lexus into the underground garage and quickly parked. She and Ricki walked up the ramp and headed toward Fountain Square.

Upon watching a homeless man shuffle around, Ricki felt a strange emptiness in her stomach. She was reminded of her recent windfall. *A ton of money just fell in my lap when I won the lottery. I could literally buy a whole chain of elegant restaurants…and this poor man has to beg for a sandwich.*

Liz nudged Ricki by the elbow. "Come on, honey, let's go," she said.

The two women approached the entrance to JTST. Liz pulled out Jeremy's security card. "I hope this thing still works!" she said. Green light. "Yes!" This was a side entrance that Jeremy often used to bypass the main security check in station. Now they wouldn't have to explain anything to the guards. They skirted down a narrow hallway and headed for the elevator.

"Let's go talk to Jeremy's business partners," Liz said. "Maybe we'll get some answers."

————

As they walked into the suite, they were greeted by a middle-aged receptionist named Marie.

"Hello, welcome to JTST. How are you ladies today?" Marie asked.

"Fine, thanks," Liz answered as she extended her right hand. "I'm Jay's sister, Liz."

The woman looked at her strangely as they shook hands.

"Oh…" Liz continued. "I mean Jeremy's sister. Jay is just his family nickname."

Upon hearing this, Marie smiled warmly. "Well, it's certainly nice to meet you," she said as she rose to her feet and shook hands again.

"And this is my friend, Ricki Valentes." Ricki extended her hand to Marie and said hello.

"Can I get coffee for either of you?" Marie asked. Both women agreed and Marie led them to a nearby conference room.

"Have a seat in here and I'll be right back with your coffees."

When Marie stepped away, Ricki gazed around the conference room. "Nice rich mahogany conference table," she commented. "And look at these nice leather chairs with the high backs. Your brother sure spared no expense here."

"You're right about that. Little brother sure must be doing something right." Liz said. Then she looked across the conference room and saw a large built-in wall cabinet. So she walked over and tugged on some of the drawers.

The top drawer was locked but the second one wasn't, so she pulled it open and glanced at a couple of files. She scanned through them quickly since Marie would be back with the coffees. Then Liz removed one of the interesting files, shut the drawer, and returned to her seat next to Ricki. She bent over and slipped the file into her purse.

Seconds later, Marie returned to the conference room with a small chrome platter containing two coffees, crème, sugar, and pastries.

After a few minutes of small talk, Marie started the conversation. "So how is Jeremy doing this week?"

"I'd like to say he's improving," Liz responded with concern in her voice. "But still not much change. The coma is consuming Jeremy at the moment."

"That's such a shame," Marie agreed. "We're all praying for him here at work."

"I really appreciate that," Liz said. "Jeremy's been bombarded with flowers. And I have collected all of his get well cards for when he awakens."

"Have the doctors given you any indication of how long the coma will last?"

"Unfortunately not," Liz answered. "From the sketchy information I have been able to piece together from the medical people, it is case by case. His doctors say it could be either very short-term or very long. No one knows for sure."

Marie looked downward and shook her head slowly in dismay. "That's exactly what we've been hearing. No one has given us a timetable for his recovery."

"Yes, that's definitely the hard part," Liz continued. She heard her phone buzz in her purse but ignored it. She continued the discussion. "Can I ask you a few questions about my brother's business?"

"Sure. What can I tell you?" Marie answered.

"What does he do daily?"

"Well, you probably know that he serves clients in stocks, bonds, ETFs, and mutuals."

"Oh, I think I knew that. Where does he get his prospects?"

"Well, each wealth manager has a base of say ten or fifteen major clients and many minor ones. Mr. Staymour meets with clients here at the office, at their place of business, or sometimes over Zoom."

"I see…what else does he do on a typical day?"

"Well, Jeremy is very talented in the area of portfolio management. As a financial advisor, everyone he meets is a perspective client."

"That makes sense," Liz answered.

"Yes. If they meet on the golf course, in a grocery, in the neighborhood, it doesn't matter. Virtually everyone has certain amounts of money to invest, and some of them have generational wealth."

"So does he mostly chase after rich people?"

"Surprisingly not," Marie answered. "The little old lady on the corner may have just received an estate check from her ninety-year-old uncle who died and had no other family. We are taught not to profile people, especially by their appearance alone."

"I guess you're right about that," Liz agreed. "Wealthy people are not always dressed in thousand-dollar suits."

Liz took a sip of coffee and then continued. "Can you tell me anything about the day my brother was shot near the Fountain? Any idea of who would want to shoot him?"

"That has us baffled. While Mr. Staymour is a Type A, he's the nicest guy you would ever meet. It just doesn't add up."

"Did he have any enemies?"

"I sure don't know of any," Marie answered. "But he did act a little out of character a few days before the incident."

"How's that?" Liz asked.

"He received many calls and seemed nervous about something. That was unusual for Jeremy since he's normally very confident."

"Did he tell anyone what was bothering him?"

"No, he's been private about his calls the last few weeks."

"Did you overhear any names of the callers?" Liz asked anxiously.

Marie thought for a moment. "Let's see…I can't recall anything out of the ord—no, wait, there was one. I overheard him call one guy…his initials were LD. I have no idea what the initials stood for. Whenever LD called, Jeremy usually walked into his office and closed the door to talk privately."

Ricki wrote that down for future reference. "Did Jeremy talk to any other people the last week or so?" Ricki interjected. "Do any names jump out at you?"

Marie thought for a moment and then responded. "There were a couple of race car drivers that he called quite often. When one of them called back, I noticed a North Carolina area code on the caller ID."

"Interesting," Liz said as she took a few more notes. "Well, we need to get going. If you think of anybody else, could you give me a call?" Liz asked as she handed Marie a business card. "Please call me on my cell."

"Sure will, Ms. Staymour. And I hope I have helped."

"Oh, you have," Liz said.

As Ricki and Liz rose from the table, they thanked Marie, shared a few final words, and left. On the way toward the lobby, Ricki turned to Liz.

"Did you get anything out of that?"

"Not a whole lot, but it was a start," Liz replied. She didn't want to tell Ricki yet, but Liz had a good idea who LD was. She couldn't wait to get home to see if her suspicion was correct.

14

A BREAK-IN AT RICKI'S HOUSE

The next morning there was a room full of people. LD blew cigar smoke and gazed around the room. Three of his goons were in attendance—a heavy man nicknamed Bruno, a tall man named Garrett, and Stokely.

LD shut the door and the meeting began promptly at Eight AM. At the end of the long oval conference table was a laptop computer. Stokely operated the keyboard as the slides were projected on the large screen at the other end of the room. The first photo on the screen showed Jeremy Staymour walking on Fountain Square.

"As all of you know by now," LD began, "this bastard is costing me millions."

The goons nodded in unison as LD continued.

"Everything was fine until young Jeremy started prying into my business. He found out about the J-36 exchange in Argentina and the Banta-38 in Jamaica. Lord only knows if the little punk stumbled across any of our bond market dealings."

LD nodded and then Stokely pressed a button. The next slide contained a picture and bio of Ricki Valentes. She looked very attractive in a form-fitting V-neck sweater and tight designer jeans.

"Whoa," Bruno shouted excitedly. "Now that's a looker!"

"Pick up your jaws, gentlemen!" LD lashed out. Bruno ducked his head in shame and LD continued. "This little hottie is the area's latest lottery winner. She's worth 39 million dollars, gentlemen." The goons became re-engaged once again.

LD blew a puff of cigar smoke and continued pacing around the oval table. "Little Ms. Ricki just happens to have a large ETF transaction with JTST." There was silence in the room for about ten seconds. LD repeated his steps behind the others who were still seated at attention around the table. He paused for emphasis, then continued speaking.

"Luckily," he began, "the Valentes transaction was halted. All of Staymour's new investments are *pending* by the feds because of the shooting on Fountain Square."

LD took a few more steps and then re-addressed his goons. "We need the thirty-nine mil, gentlemen! Is that clear?" The robots nodded in unison. Their fear of the old man was quite apparent and he preferred it that way. Intimidation was his strength.

The next person on the screen was Daniel Flarity. LD glanced over at Bruno, who anxiously awaited an assignment.

"Hey Bruno, do me a favor, huh?"

"Yes, boss?"

"Bring me this guy, Flarity."

Bruno smiled and salivated at the challenge. "Can I rough him up, boss…you know, just for the hell of it?"

"Bruno, there'll be a time and a place for that," LD shot back. "But not this time. Just bring him to me, my boy."

Bruno looked down disappointedly. "Okay, boss, Flarity's mine." After a few closing remarks, the meeting adjourned.

————

Liz walked through the reception area of County Memorial and checked in with the guard. The elevator was being repaired, so she took the stairs to Jeremy's floor. She approached Mrs. McNamara, the receptionist, who was ending a call. Mrs. McNamara saw Liz and spoke first.

"Oh, hello Ms. Staymour, how are you doing?"

"Not bad. What's the latest with Jeremy? Getting any better?"

"He's still in stable condition," the receptionist replied. "Dr. Kingsbury can tell you more. Shall I page him for you?"

"Well I can't see him right now," Liz answered. "I have a meeting with Nurse Curtis. Have you seen her this morning?"

"She's headed this way now," Mrs. McNamara answered while pointing down the hall. Liz turned and smiled as she spotted a woman in hospital attire.

―――

Liz smiled at Nurse Curtis and they exchanged pleasantries. then headed for a nearby conference room. Nurse Curtis closed the door and they each pulled out chairs. They shared some more small talk and laughed a little. Then Liz opened her notepad and turned toward Nurse Curtis.

"Well, Angie, there's something I've discovered about Jeremy." Angie raised her eyebrows with sudden curiosity.

"And what's that?" Nurse Curtis asked.

"When I visited my brother's business the other day, his associates acted suspiciously—almost as if they were hiding something."

"That's strange, I wonder what?" Nurse Curtis asked.

"I'm not sure. But I did some snooping around and I found a few notes in one of Jeremy's file drawers. There was a printed email from some guy named Rajo, or something like that."

She thought for a second and then it came to her. "His last name was Spanish sounding. It was Soy something." She hesitated a few seconds and then it came to her. "Soyamos, yeah, that was it."

Angie looked at Liz strangely and didn't know what to say. Then Liz spoke again.

"Doesn't sound like your average American, does it?"

"No, sure doesn't," Nurse Curtis agreed. Liz pulled out a few more notes that she had "borrowed" from her brother's files.

"And then I found these." She laid an email message and two photographs on the table. I think the guy's from Argentina."

"So your brother's doing some international business," Angie said. "What's so strange about that?"

"My thoughts exactly...until I read this paragraph," Liz countered as she handed the note to Angie who immediately began reading:

Dear Mr. Staymour:

Thanks to you for meeting with me yesterday. I hope you were happy with our new investments. We trade on the J-36 SE every day. Our insurance is the S. American coalition—very respectable down here. Please say if you plan to come down, and I'll walk with you.

Rajo

Nurse Curtis rolled her eyes. "Definitely some broken English, but the message is still coherent." She paused and continued. "I wonder what your brother's involved in? Sounds shady."

"I'm not sure," Liz answered with a sigh. "But I'm going to do some more digging. I want to make sure this Rajo character is legit."

"Just curious, why are you sharing this with me?" Angie asked. "I'm only your brother's nurse."

"You're more than that to me, Nurse Curtis. I feel like I've known you for years."

"But—"

"Don't but me," Liz interrupted playfully. She stood up from the table and walked over and embraced Nurse Curtis.

"My brother is quite possibly in some deep shit." She paused a moment, raised her sorrowful eyebrows, then continued. "Could you help me investigate this more?"

Nurse Curtis held Liz's hand in hers and smiled with affirmation.

Liz continued talking. "And since you are here at the hospital, and you've been so helpful, I—"

"Don't say any more," Nurse Curtis interrupted. "I'd be glad to help."

Liz wiped away a tear and the two women hugged again. A few seconds later, Angie asked, "So…how can I help?"

"Please keep an eye out for any suspicious characters trying to make their way into Jeremy's room. Also, be suspicious of any inquiries about my brother."

"I'd be glad to," Nurse Curtis answered with another smile.

"Thanks," Liz replied. "It's nice to have such a good friend."

The two women said their goodbyes and departed the conference room.

———

As Liz walked toward the hospital lobby, she pulled out her cell and made a quick call to Ricki. The phone rang three times.

"Hello?"

"Ricki, it's Liz. Just wondered if I could stop by."

"Sure, I was just—hold on, someone's at the door."

Liz listened intently through her phone. She heard Ricki talking to someone, and it was a male.

"Hey, what are you doing to my door?" Ricki yelled through the closed door. Then she saw a crowbar prying through.

"What the fuck are you doing?" Ricki yelled fearfully. Liz strained to hear the commotion through her cell. A crashing noise and a slamming door. Seconds later, Liz heard more male voices followed by a woman's scream.

"Ricki!" Liz yelled into her phone, "Are you okay?" She heard more rustling, so Liz shouted again through her cell:

"Ricki! Ricki, are you okay? Please say something!"

A few seconds later, a man's voice was on the other end.

"She's just fine," the man said mockingly. Liz heard some evil laughter from a couple of men and then the phone just went dead.

"Ricki!" Liz screamed louder. But there was no response. An agitated Liz hung up and sprinted to her car. She couldn't believe what she had just heard!

It was a thirty-minute drive to Ricki's house. Liz felt helpless and wondered what to do next. Finally, she decided to drive there herself.

While exiting the driveway, Liz reported the incident to 9-1-1.

"Hello, I'd like to report a break-in," Liz began.

"One moment please," the emergency operator placed the call on hold.

"Son of a bitch," Liz yelled out. She shook her head in disgust and pounded her fist on her steering wheel. "What could happen next?!"

Liz mumbled a few more cuss words while she waited on hold. She drove a half mile further and the Emergency operator had still not returned to the line. Now Liz was miffed so she ended the call and tossed the cell on the passenger's seat.

Seconds later, she remembered having Detective Lankford's business card. She reached for the strap of her purse, but the purse fell to the floor.

"Damn it!" she yelled. Frustrated, she pulled the Lexus to the shoulder and slowed the car to a stop. She turned on her flashers and then reached for the fallen purse on the floor.

Liz riffled through the credit cards in her wallet and located the wrinkled business card. She grabbed her cell and waited for the connection.

"Lankford."

"Hello, Detective. This is Liz Staymour. You're not going to believe what just happened."

"What now?"

"I was on the phone with Ricki Valentes and I heard a struggle. Someone broke into her home!"

"Oh no. Is she okay?"

"I don't know. I heard some loud male voices, a scream. Then one of the creeps came on the phone and made a wisecrack. He said Ricki was just fine, and then he laughed along with the others. A few seconds later the line went dead."

"Sounds like a gang of some sort," Lankford answered. "Thanks for the information, Ms. Staymour. I'll send a cruiser to Ms. Valentes' house immediately." He paused. "Second thought, I'll go there myself."

15

DETECTIVE LANKFORD TO THE SCENE

Detective Lankford drove wildly with his blue emergency lights on, but no siren. He was en route to Ricki Valentes' house to investigate the break-in. Acting on Liz's tip, he hoped that it wasn't too late.

He pulled into Ricki's driveway and perused the house and porch. The storm door was bent off of the hinges. He skidded to a stop and quickly hopped out.

When he reached the porch, Lankford spotted blood stains on the door frame. "Damn," he mumbled. He slipped his gloves on and observed the gap in the door frame. Grooved and splintered. Lankford's stomach churned, and he hoped Ricki was still alive.

The detective pushed over the broken door and stepped through the opening to the living room. With his gun drawn, Lankford took a few more steps. He was careful in case the intruder was still inside.

"Ricki…are you here?" Lankford yelled while aiming the gun in front of him. No answer.

Lankford's eyes moved back and forth as he walked toward the center of the room. He quickly decided to check the rest of the house for the intruder. Gun still drawn, the detective surveyed each room, but there was still no sign of Ricki.

Seconds later, CSI investigators arrived. They greeted Lankford, and then went about their business. "Any sign of Valentes?" one of them asked.

"No, the house is clear," Lankford answered. He took a second trip through the living room to search for evidence. A lamp had been knocked over and was lying sideways on the sofa. As Lankford continued to investigate the scene, he spotted a small bloodstain on the arm of the sofa.

"Over here!" he yelled to one of the technicians. A young woman knelt and carefully observed the red stain. She took out a small knife and cut a swatch of the sofa. It appeared to contain blood. She carefully placed it in a zip-lock baggie and labeled the evidence with a sharpie.

Detective Lankford unhooked his radio from his shoulder strap and reported to the precinct.

"This is Lankford."

"Yes, sir," the woman dispatcher replied. "What's your ten-twenty?"

"I'm at 754 Lakeview. I secured the premises. There's no sign of the perp or Ms. Valentes." There was a momentary silence while the dispatcher typed the information.

"Did you copy that?" the detective asked impatiently. A few seconds later, the dispatcher confirmed.

"Yes, copy."

"Okay, thanks." The detective pushed the standby button and returned the radio to the clip on his shoulder.

———

An urgent meeting was led by LD. Like usual, the husky man was puffing on a Cuban cigar and pacing around the conference table. "You dumb asses!" he lashed out. "Why did you bring me the Valentes broad? I told you to get Flarity!" The goons were embarrassed and speechless. Finally, Stokely spoke up.

"I'll take the hit for this, boss," he began. LD's bushy eyebrows arose instinctively and his eyes peered angrily at him. Before the big man could pounce, Stokely continued his lame explanation of the events.

"Boss, it all happened quickly. Flarity's car was in the driveway, and the broad's car was gone. So we assumed he was home alone."

LD blew a smoke ring and appeared to be only half-listening. The others in the room looked around nervously. There was a pause in the conversation and then LD walked behind Stokely, who was still seated at the table.

LD, the *intimidator*, was back. The old man bent down and blew a big puff of cigar smoke at Stokely. The nervous man squirmed in his chair and struggled to think clearly.

"So then what?" LD lashed out. Stokely flinched slightly then responded quickly.

"We busted into the home and hoped to find Flarity. Instead, his rich little bimbo was there."

"How much am I paying you clowns?" LD fired back at all of them. The goons all sat dejectedly with their heads down.

"What should we do with her now, boss?" Bruno asked.

LD just shook his head and paced a few steps around the table. A few seconds later, he responded. "Blindfold her and take her for a ride," LD began. "Take her to Leo's ranch. But keep her alive, you fools! The broad's worth millions."

The three goons stood in unison. LD lashed out again. "And remember, bring me Flarity...shall I spell his name for you, gentlemen?" LD yelled as he coughed on his cigar smoke. The goons headed quickly for the door to begin their new mission.

———

Liz was worried sick. Just four hours earlier, she had advised Detective Lankford of her horrifying phone call with Ricki. Was

Ricki okay? What the hell was going on? Liz deliberated for a few more moments and then decided against calling Lankford again—at least not yet. The police are working on it, she assured herself.

She opened the refrigerator. "Damn it!" she said. "I'm not even hungry." Food was the last thing on her mind at the moment. Her family was in complete disarray. Jeremy was a vegetable locked inside a never-ending coma! Then trouble continued to follow Liz. She was shocked to hear that her new friend Ricki was beaten and kidnapped from her home. What could happen next?

All of this was starting to weigh on Liz. She shut the refrigerator door, turned to pick up her cell, and tapped the number. After a few rings, Angie Curtis answered.

"Hello?" the nurse began.

"Angie, it's Liz Staymour. Do you have a few minutes?"

"Oh, sure Liz. What's up?"

"Do you remember Ricki Valentes?"

"The lottery winner?"

"Yeah, it was surreal," Liz continued. "I was talking to her on the phone and I heard a loud banging noise through the receiver."

"You're kidding! What happened? Is Ricki okay?"

"Someone broke into her house while she was on the phone with me," Liz answered.

"That's nuts," Angie commented. "Then what happened?"

"Well, I kept screaming her name and I heard some rustling on the other end. I wanted to leap through the phone and help her."

"You're kidding! So what did you do?"

"Well I continued calling out for Ricki, but the phone went dead, so I called the police detective."

"I can't believe it!" Angie said. "I didn't think Ricki had any enemies. What did the authorities tell you?"

"They're still investigating," Liz said. "I'm waiting to get anything positive out of them."

"Wow," Angie said softly with concern in her voice. "I hope she's okay."

"Me too," Liz responded. "It may have something to do with Jeremy."

16

A DREAM AND A KIDNAPPING

Jeremy slept peacefully within the depths of the coma until the dream began. Like other dreams while comatose, Jeremy found himself flying high over various neighborhoods. He saw a huge, red radio tower with flashing lights.

He flew like a dove, glanced downward, and whizzed by a chain of stores. A highway patrolman aimed his radar gun down the entrance ramp of I-75.

Still dreaming, Jeremy's spirit drifted over downtown Cincinnati. He flew over the Carew Tower, the city's tallest building. Some tourists milled around on the building's rooftop observation deck. A father helped his son look through a huge telescope at the sites below.

The feeling was so tranquil. There was no pain, only calmness. Next, Jeremy's spirit flew over Great American Ballpark, where an afternoon ballgame was underway. The dream continued as he flew over the John Roebling Suspension Bridge. What was happening near the river? He couldn't tell. There was a traffic jam on the bridge.

Some motorists were standing outside of their cars and pointing at the riverbank down below.

Suddenly, the dream began to fade. *No! Don't fade. I want to see what's happening!* The human figures flickered and the voices suddenly faded.

Next, Jeremy heard footsteps approaching. Seconds later, he felt his bed sheet being pulled up to his chin. Someone tucked him in for the evening. The dream was over, but the coma continued.

———

The voice in Jeremy's head offered encouraging words. *"Sleep tight, young Jeremy, and remain strong. I'll help you fight this thing."*

Jeremy tried to have faith…tried to believe everything his conscience was telling him. After a slight pause, Jeremy answered. *"You've got it! I'll be strong."*

For a few seconds, Jeremy didn't hear anything. And then the voice returned. *"Okay, partner. I'm counting on you. I'll snap you out of this—even if it takes a lifetime."*

The corner of Jeremy's lip moved as he tried to smile. *"I hope you're right. I hate lying here in limbo!"*

———

Daniel Flarity left work early when he couldn't reach Ricki. He had been texting her all morning but had received no replies. Next, he tried her cell but only got her voicemail. He was perplexed about her recent disappearances.

While driving to her home, Daniel felt an increased anxiety level. He somehow reeled himself in and re-focused on the road. Seconds later, he saw a strange car in his rearview mirror. It was a big car—a dark Lincoln. Daniel returned his eyes to the road for just a few seconds when the Lincoln passed him. Seconds later, there were two trucks on his tail.

"Jesus! You idiots!" All of this was taking place on a single-lane road with no escape route. The driver of the rust-colored truck accelerated and quickly caught up with Daniel's Honda Accord. The truck tapped the Accord once in the rear, then crashed into it harder, causing Daniel's car to swerve a little.

Suddenly, the Lincoln driver laid on the brakes and came to a sudden crawl. Daniel had no option but to stop as well. Four men jumped out of the Lincoln and the rear cars and stormed his vehicle. One man yanked the driver's door, pulled Daniel to the ground, and slammed him twice with a wooden club.

Another man placed a handkerchief over his nose and waited for the drugs to take effect. The assaulters dragged Daniel's limp body to the Lincoln, stuffed him into the back, and stormed off. As Daniel drifted into a light sleep, he heard one of the men.

"We've got him, boss. What should we do with the merchandise?"

———

Late that afternoon, Detective Lankford received a report of an abduction on State Route 73 near Waynesville. The roads are very curvy and wooded in the Waynesville area. The report documented the conversation. It stated that a hunter was crossing the road and witnessed everything.

"A big, dark car forced a smaller car to the side of the road. Two men got out of the big car, ran over, and yanked the other guy out of his car!" the hunter reported by cell to the station. "They clubbed the hell out of him, picked him up, and threw him in their car."

"What kind of car was it? The dispatcher asked."

"A Lincoln."

"Then what?"

"They just sped off and left the guy's car in the middle of the road."

Lankford shook his head in disbelief. Just what he needed to hear—a beating and another kidnapping. The real shocker came when he read an updated bulletin that had just been handed to him. The name of the hostage was very familiar—Daniel Flarity.

Of all the people to disappear, this was the worst-case scenario—first a thirty-nine-million-dollar lottery winner disappears and then her boyfriend follows suit!

"Great," Lankford murmured sarcastically. "First Ricki Valentes then Daniel Flarity."

The phone rang and the detective picked it up. "This is Lankford."

"Hi Daddy," the young voice began. "When are you coming home?" It was Lankford's young daughter, Sara.

"Soon, honey. Daddy will be coming home soon."

"You promised to read me my book," she begged.

"I will, I will, honey. I promise. I'll be home soon." Then Lankford heard his wife's voice in the background whispering to the child.

"Okay Daddy," Sara answered. "I love you."

"I love you too, snookums. Now put mommy on the phone."

Lankford smiled as he thought about his adorable young daughter. When his wife came on the line, he assured her he would be home in an hour.

———

Ricki was groggy but slowly regaining consciousness. Her head was pounding like a kettledrum. Where am I, and how did I get here? Seated on a cold tile floor, she found herself bound, gagged, and blindfolded. Her heart rate accelerated as extreme panic set in. She screamed at the top of her lungs, but her muffled cries were heard by no one. Her saliva soaked through the ragged cloth that gagged her mouth.

Still panicking, she rolled to her side and rubbed her face back and forth on the floor in an attempt to remove the gag. Work it loose!

After ten long minutes of squirming and repeating the maneuver, she paused, realizing she was making very little progress.

The gag was as tight as ever, causing her lips to bleed profusely. She rested for a few more minutes to clear her mind. She pondered her options, but she had no escape plan.

A minute later, panic resurfaced. She screamed a few more times but her efforts were fruitless. Her head pounded worse than before. Five more minutes seemed more like five hours. Ricki was so mentally exhausted that she passed out again.

At some point in the evening, Ricki awoke to the sound of loud footsteps approaching. She heard keys jingling just before the door flew open. Two men entered the room and slammed the door behind them.

———

"Take off her blindfold!" one of the men ordered. The shorter man bent down and untied the blindfold. Ricki opened her eyes and tried to focus on the strange men.

"Now, if you can behave yourself, Ms. Valentes, we'll remove your gag. Can we trust you?"

Ricki nodded her head in approval and the shorter man untied the gag. Ricki gasped for air and then lashed out at her captors.

"Who are you assholes? And what do you want?" Ricki glared. When there was no response, she screamed a few more obscenities.

The two men laughed as they watched their victim struggle in vain. Seconds later, she rocked from side to side in a futile attempt to loosen the ropes that bound her wrists and ankles.

"Please take these damned ropes off!" she pleaded. "They're stopping my circulation."

The men laughed again and left the room. They slammed and locked the door behind them. Their conversation faded as they walked further down the hall. Exasperated, Ricki searched for answers. *Who are these creeps…and what do they want from me?*

The pain was excruciating. Her hands and feet throbbed. *Why?* she wondered. *It's the money they want—thirty or forty million dollars…*

Tears flowed down the face of the multi-millionaire. There would be no extravagant homes, nice cars, or European vacations. First she would have to survive this ordeal. "They're not getting one penny!" she screamed in vain. "They'll have to kill me first!"

Before falling asleep, she wracked her brain some more, hoping to discover a way out.

———

When Ricki awoke, she was met with a surprise. Seated next to her was a blindfolded man.

"Oh my gosh! Daniel, what are you doing here?"

.

17

COMA BLUES AND A VISIT WITH LANKFORD

Liz held her comatose brother's limp hand. At the same time, Nurse Angie gently lifted Jeremy's left eyelid and squirted a few drops of saline over his cornea. She repeated the process on his right eye.

"That should keep him for a while," she commented. "We must keep his eyes moist."

Not hearing a word just spoken by her friend, Liz grieved over her brother's unresponsive condition. *It's like he's already dead. His heart is beating like a drum, and his breathing seems normal through the respirator, but he won't wake up. He's lying there like a vegetable!*

Liz wanted to shake him by the shoulders to awaken him. She wished it were that easy. She stared at him some more then whispered, "I love you, Jay." She bent over and kissed him gently on the forehead.

The nurse prepared a treatment for Jeremy and turned to say something to Liz. Before getting another word out, Angie saw that Liz had tears streaming down her face. Angie walked over and put her arm around her friend to comfort her.

"I know it's tough to see him like this," Angie began. Liz returned the embrace and sobbed on the nurse's shoulder. "It's just not fair," Liz said. "He doesn't deserve this."

Angie comforted her friend for a few more seconds, then gently patted her shoulder. "I know it's tough. Hang in there, honey." She handed Liz a tissue.

"Thanks, Angie. I'm going to think positively. Jay will get through this ordeal."

There was a short pause for reflection. Then Liz gently rubbed her brother's forehead. "You've always been a fighter, buddy. I'll be right here when you wake up."

Angie helped Liz to her feet, paused a few seconds, then both women turned and headed out the door.

————

Jeremy was in the REM cycle within the coma. Trapped behind prison walls in one respect, he had to find a way out—get back to the conscious world. But he knew that he held information that LD and his thugs were seeking. Jeremy knew some information about LD's business dealings with an Argentinian company. *LD can't afford for me to take this information to the grave!*

Everything seemed to fade in and out. It was like a "This is your life" slow-motion video. He saw visions of his childhood where he was playing with army men in the sandbox.

Just as he was pouring water from a bucket into the sand, his mind switched to a frightful water event when he slipped underwater in a neighbor's pool and nearly drowned before being saved by his father. The near-drowning re-occurrence seemed so vivid, that Jeremy gasped for air from within the coma.

The next vision was a scene with four or five shadowy figures. As Jeremy "focused," he saw shadows of men in business suits. A discussion around a huge brown oval table.

The men's faces went in and out of focus. Thick, cloudy cigar smoke arose slowly over the table. The circular light overhead was a fuzzy halo.

LD, what are you planning? Jeremy lashed out. *You sent Kinsey to poison me, but he FAILED! Yes, I'm still alive.*

In the vision, he tried to move his eyes to peruse the room. But the scene went in and out of focus. Blurry, sharper, and then blurry again. Jeremy's head pounded and soon he nodded off to sleep.

––––––

When Jeremy awoke from his nap, he felt better. At least the headache went away. When his charts were up-to-date, Nurse Curtis had an idea. Her research and experience told her that comatose patients are not just lying there sleeping. Most studies suggest that coma patients are aware of their surroundings and need mental stimulation to hasten recovery. Nurse Curtis skimmed the headlines and read Jeremy some news stories from her iPhone.

"You're not going to believe this one, Mr. Staymour. Seven masked men broke into a high-end apparel store today in a crowded mall and stole a half million dollars' worth of imported purses."

Nurse Angie looked up momentarily from her phone and thought she saw a slight smirk on Jeremy's face.

Boy, the nerve of these crooks. Right in the middle of broad daylight, a smash and grab! Where was the rental cop? Was our infamous Officer Wilson working there? Jeremy joked from within the coma.

Angie couldn't hear Jeremy's silent rants, but she probably would have appreciated his humor about Wilson.

————

Liz visited Detective Lankford at the precinct for a follow-up discussion about Ricki. They discussed more details about the lottery winner's abduction.

"I still can't believe she was kidnapped!" Liz began. "I was talking to her on the phone and I heard the commotion in the background."

"So tell me again what you heard," Lankford probed. "How many voices were there?"

"I heard crashing noises and maybe a crowbar hitting the floor. There were two or three voices, all males." Liz paused while Lankford poured her some more coffee. She took a sip before continuing. "Wow, that's good coffee!"

"Thanks, I just ground the beans this morning. What else did you hear?"

"Well there was shouting and then Ricki screamed."

"Did you recognize any of the voices?"

"Unfortunately no."

"Hmmm," Lankford mumbled as he scribbled a few notes. "How is your relationship with Ricki? I realize you have only known her for a short time."

"Yeah, I introduced myself to her a few weeks ago. I was fascinated to meet a lottery winner!"

"Yes, I recall from the news story," Lankford said as he glanced up from his notebook. "I forgot the exact amount."

"Thirty-nine million. Can you imagine winning that much?"

"Nope, but I'd like to try!" Lankford commented. "That lucky woman's set for generations."

"Yeah, but that kind of wealth attracts vultures," Liz commented as she rolled her eyes.

"Unfortunately," Lankford mumbled with his head still buried in his notes. "Root of all evil." He paused to sip his coffee. "Has Ricki opened an account at your brother's company?"

Liz hesitated about telling Lankford this information, but then she realized that many general details had already been leaked to the press. Finally, she responded, "Well, I'm still researching the details, but a large investment transaction may be in process."

That got the attention of Lankford. "In process?"

"Yes," she continued. "Ricki opened a large portfolio at JTST but the funds are listed as *pending*."

"Oh, really?"

"Yes. The SEC has paused all of JTST's new setups until the Fed completes its investigation of the shooting."

"So Ricki's multi-million-dollar windfall is only *pending*? In limbo?" Lankford repeated in amazement.

Liz nodded and finished her coffee.

Lankford rubbed his balding head. "Okay, that's good to know, but I'll hold off putting it in the report until we confirm," Lankford replied.

"Probably a good idea," Liz responded. "Bullets are flying and people are disappearing."

"That's true," Lankford said. He flipped back a page in his notebook.

"So let's see if I have the chronology straight: Your brother is a wealth manager who was shot in a drive-by on Fountain Square, knocking him into a coma. When they discovered Jeremy survived, someone snuck into his hospital room and tried to poison him. Someone ran your car off the road and luckily you survived. Over thirty million dollars of Ricki Valentes's money is in limbo at JTST. Then recently, Ricki and her boyfriend, Daniel Flarity, were kidnapped in separate instances. However, we think the same thugs are holding both victims."

Lankford frowned at Liz in disbelief and asked if he had captured everything.

"You've got it," she said. "The whole thing's crazy!"

18

ASTONISHMENT AT COUNTY MEMORIAL

Down at County Memorial, Nurse Curtis was performing a routine exam on Jeremy. As she had done many times, the nurse leaned forward and spoke to him. "So Jeremy, how are you feeling today?"

Jeremy's eyes were slightly hazed. He stared straight ahead like he had done every day since his arrival in the ICU. The blank stare continued as expected. But then his eyelids lowered and opened slowly. A few seconds later, a couple of more blinks. Then he murmured something! "Uhhhh."

Hearing this, Nurse Curtis was intrigued. Could this be a miracle? She patted his shoulder gently and whispered encouragement. "Talk to me, Jeremy. What would you like to tell me?"

After another pause, Jeremy blinked and made two more muffled noises.

Nurse Curtis was so excited, she pressed a button on her pager and summoned additional medical staff. A passing doctor and two women nurses immediately came running to see what the commotion was all about.

"Look, his eyes are staying open and he is making noises," Angie began. Everyone looked on with bated breath. Then the doctor bent down and spoke to Jeremy. "Hello there, I'm Dr. Campbell. Can you see or hear me?" Still no response. "Squeeze my hand, Jeremy, if you hear me."

The patient's limp fingers were lying on Dr. Campbell's hand but there was no movement. "Jeremy, Jeremy," the doctor repeated softly.

"Can you please squeeze my hand?"

Suddenly it happened—Jeremy squeezed very softly and a few seconds later, an even harder squeeze. The nurses stared in amazement and their eyes moistened.

"Good job, Jeremy," Dr. Campbell continued. Jeremy's eyes moved leftward, then slowly rightward as he surveyed the room. He saw shadowy figures and a fuzzy light overhead. Jeremy was trying to focus. His lips quivered, and he looked like he wanted to speak. *Where am I?* He thought. *Is this real… or just another hallucination?*

"Jeremy, wiggle your shoulder if you can see me clearly?" the doctor said. Nothing. Then the doctor tried again. Still nothing. Then a third time. "Jeremy, is your vision clearing?" Seconds later, Jeremy lifted his right shoulder.

"Alright!" Nurse Curtis yelled. The medical staff in the room gave high fives as they erupted with excitement. Three more nurses joined in a group hug as well.

Smiling brightly, Dr. Campbell turned to the staff and said, "We'll continue with more testing this afternoon. In the meantime, tell his family the good news!"

————

Angie tapped the number into her cell. "Miss Staymour, it's Nurse Curtis at the hospital."

"Oh hello, how's it going?"

"Doing great. Well, the day has finally come. Jeremy has responded to questions by clenching the doctor's fist! It appears he can see and hear."

"You're kidding me! That's wonderful!" Liz replied with joy in her eyes. "I can't believe it! Can he talk too?

"No, not yet," the nurse responded.

"That's okay. Does this mean he is out of the coma?" she asked excitedly. As she stood too quickly, Liz accidentally knocked over her kitchen chair and it nearly hit her cat.

"These are very early stages, but it's looking a lot better, "Angie stated. "The doctors are thrilled with his progress."

Liz's heart pounded with excitement for her brother. "I'm so excited. What's next? How soon will he be talking again?"

"Not sure. The doctors have called a meeting to discuss the next steps. We'll have to wait and see."

———

Dr. Campbell and Nurse Curtis met with Liz and her boyfriend, Heath. The four of them shuffled into a conference room to discuss a rehab program for Jeremy.

After the introductions and small talk, Dr. Campbell stood and spoke first. "Hello. Thanks for coming at short notice. Here is what Jeremy will be facing in recovery. Because of the six-month length of the coma, Jeremy has experienced severe muscle loss and it will be a couple of weeks before he can walk without assistance."

"Oh, really," Liz said. I knew there would be a rehab program."

Then, Dr. Campbell continued. "Because Jeremy had his days and nights mixed up while in the coma, he will most probably suffer from psychosis. This is a condition where he may have difficulty determining what is real and not real. He may also become severely disoriented at times. Thirdly, he may become paranoid, experience anxiety, or hear voices."

"Well, that's a lot of possible symptoms, but I'll take it! Thanks for the explanation, doctor," said Liz. "At least we'll know what he's up against."

"Yes, it is best to stay positive and show support for your brother," the doctor advised. "We'll reassess him in a couple of weeks. Any questions, just let us know."

All four people arose and left the conference room.

———

Three days later, Dr. Campbell met with Jeremy and discussed rehab and recovery. Then Nurse Curtis wheeled the patient down to the second floor and they toured the entire rehab facility.

"Tomorrow will be your first day of rehab, Jeremy. Any questions?" Nurse Curtis asked.

"No Ma'am. Thanks," he murmured softly His eyes were heavy and he was still very groggy.

19

RUN FOR THE WOODS

Blindfolded and feeling helpless, Ricki and Daniel were still being held hostage. Their wrists bound tightly with rope, they sat back to back in steel chairs. Daniel nodded off for about ten minutes. But Ricki rubbed the rope on a protruding screw on the back of her chair. Meticulously, she worked.

Back and forth, back and forth, twenty, maybe thirty times until there were only a few strings left. She pulled her wrists apart once, then twice. It was so close. She rubbed the final few threads across the nail once more and it separated. Her hands were free!

She yanked her blindfold off and untied the ropes from her feet. Turning to Daniel, she pulled his blindfold off and he struggled to focus.

"Hi Daniel, let me untie you," she said.

"How did you get your ropes off?"

"Cut the wrist rope with a stray screw on my chair."

"Oh thank God!" Daniel answered. "Let's get the hell out of here!"

So Ricki quickly untied his body, wrists, and legs. They were both free to move around now. The only problem was that the giant wood door was still double-locked from the outside. There were just two light bulbs in the room and the two glass block windows were good for allowing daylight in, but they were nearly impossible to break.

Daniel surveyed the room and analyzed the concrete walls, fortified windows, and wood door. Unfortunately, it was a very secure bunker with no way out. "We'll wait until they bring our next meal then we'll be waiting from behind the door," he said.

"Good plan, honey." Ricki looked at her watch—11:27 AM. "They usually bring lunch around 12:30, so we'll have to pay close attention to the time."

———

It was 12:20. Ricki and Daniel waited to pounce.

"Lunch should arrive in about ten or fifteen minutes."

"Yeah," Daniel said. "When we hear them coming, stand about ten feet from the door and off to the left. When the door opens, dart to the center of the room. That will distract him enough for me to strike."

Their estimate was pretty close. At 12:35, they heard approaching footsteps. When the door opened, Ricki distracted the man and then

Daniel slammed a chair on the thug's neck and shoulders causing the tray of food to fly across the room and crash to the floor.

"Uhhhhh," the man gasped. Daniel hit him with the chair a couple more times. He and Ricki escaped, slamming the door behind them.

The door had a one-way electronic lock from the outside. As the duo ran, they could hear the injured man yelling and pounding his fist on the locked door. He was stuck in his own trap.

Daniel and Ricki ran down two more hallways and finally came upon an outside door. They ran through a large meadow and looked behind them. No one was following. At least not yet.

They made it to a dense forest where Ricki doubled over to catch her breath. Seconds later, they took the first path they saw and disappeared deeper into the woods.

————

Daniel and Ricki ran past a line of oak and maple trees and hiked down an adjoining trail leading to a ravine. They walked along a trickling creek and over a wooden bridge crossing the creek.

They jogged to another trail that wound slightly and led up a hill. Then a gunshot echoed in the air. They ducked slightly when a bullet hit a tree about ten feet away. Then another shot rang out, this one striking Daniel in the knee and dropping him to the ground.

"Uhhhh," he screamed as he grabbed his knee in pain. Ricki bent down to attend to him. As she did so, another bullet whizzed by her head and struck a woodpile.

"Damn it!" she moaned. "What in the hell do these creeps want from us?" She hugged Daniel for a few seconds. Blood gushed from his thigh as he rolled in pain.

"Don't move or you're dead!" a man shouted.

Ricki looked up and saw four armed men with pistols drawn. The men shoved Ricki and Daniel on their stomachs and quickly bound their hands behind their backs.

"Now get to your feet. We're taking another walk!"

"I don't think I CAN walk," Daniel groaned.

"Well you're gonna try, you damn punk!" Ricki walked slowly. Daniel limped a step or two behind. He was in pain and was constantly shoved by the men, forcing him to continue.

A half-hour later, Daniel and Ricki found themselves in the same dim room secured by the electronic door lock. The men re-tied them in the chairs—this time with motion-sensitive electronic ankle bracelets. If either of them struggled too much, they would receive a painful shock. To make things worse, LD and his team would receive immediate notifications on their phones. A couple of thugs would come running and joyfully inflict additional pain to the captives.

———

Approaching footsteps rang out in the hall. There was a loud buzz and five men entered through the door. LD was the stocky man wearing an open-collared shirt, a brown blazer, and khaki pants. He had tattoos on his neck and chest. Two of the henchmen had numerous tattoos as well.

LD approached Daniel, stared at him for a few seconds, then circled to glare at Ricki as well. Finally, the burly man stopped at the side of them so he could begin speaking.

"So you are my two little escapees…huh?" Neither of them said a word. LD continued the circular walk and stopped in front of Daniel. "Whose idea was it to ambush my men and escape?"

To protect Ricki, Daniel spoke out. "It was my idea."

In response, LD back-handed Daniel across the face, causing an immediate bruise and bloody nose. The blow knocked Daniel to one side and pulled Ricki with him.

"Uhhhhh," he moaned.

"I should kill both of you," LD said. "But here's a good way you can save each other." He paused for a few seconds and then got face-to-face with Daniel. "I hear that your girlfriend seated behind you is a very large lottery winner…is that right?" Daniel knew what LD was driving at so he didn't answer immediately. *What do you say to this burly nut job?*

"Well, not that I—" Then one of the other henchmen laid another blow to Daniel's face, and more blood shot out of the other nostril.

"Enough!" Ricki yelled. She couldn't stand the thought of Daniel being beaten. Besides, her lottery winning was public information all over the net.

"Yes, you're right," Ricki said. "I did win the lottery, thirty-nine million back in April."

The amount matched what LD had already known. He read nearly every link describing Ricki Valentes' windfall.

Daniel's face ached and his leg throbbed. He wanted to yell an obscenity at the thug. Noticing resistance, the thug pulled his gun and quickly placed it on Daniel's temple.

"Can I shoot him, boss? I'll blow his head off right here."

"No, not yet, Bruno. As long as his rich little girlfriend cooperates."

"What? I'll do what you want!" Ricki yelled desperately. "Just stop beating Daniel!"

"Okay, here's how you can save his life and your own life so that one day you'll live to see kids and grandkids," LD began. "Go to your wealth management company, your banks, credit unions, wherever the hell you have it stashed, and withdraw all thirty-nine million."

"There is one big problem with your scheme," Ricki countered smartly. "The majority of the money is stuck in a *pending* status at JTST investments until the Feds investigate his shooting."

"That's right, damn Staymour's hanging on by a thread, and it's screwing us all up!" LD bellowed.

"So what is the split of your accounts? Write 'em down," he demanded as he handed Ricki a pen and tablet. Ricki wrote down the breakout of 36.5 Million:

JTST (pending)	*$30,502,000*
Jefferson Woodward WM	*$ 1,000,000*
Zubert Natl CU	*$ 1,000,000*
Wildwood First Fed WM	*$ 4,000,000*
TOTAL	***$36,502,000***

"What happened to the other three million?"

"I spent it as mad money!" Ricki lied. She only spent about a hundred thousand, but she hoped LD would let her keep this difference.

"Okay, well contact the bottom three and pull out six million," LD shouted disappointedly. "We'll get the rest later. Contact them by phone and wire it to our offshore account. I'll give you instructions for the wires."

"Not to be stupid," Ricki began, "but wouldn't it throw up a red flag if you wire to an off-shore account? It would surely arouse suspicion at the institutions. More forms to complete, more questions, et cetera?"

"We've taken care of that. Our bogus routing numbers are coded to fool them. The banks won't know the exact location of the transfer. The computers will show the money staying stateside."

After a short pause, LD added, "And just remember…no funny stuff! If you tip off the financial managers or the cops about any of this, your good friend Daniel here will get a shiny bullet in the middle of his forehead!"

At that moment, a dark-haired handsome man walked into the room. Ricki had so much on her mind about losing her fortune, that she was looking downward to concentrate. When she looked up, she was shocked at what she saw.

"Hello, Ricki," the man said with a cocky smile. *Oh my God,* Ricki thought, *it's Kent, the Minneapolis guy.* The fact that the man knew Ricki made Daniel suspicious. "You know that guy?" he asked angrily. Ricki responded half-heartedly.

"Kind of, but not really. He was stalking me in Minnesota. Now it's making more sense."

Kent stood behind Daniel. He smiled at Ricki, but he didn't contradict her story.

She continued speaking. "I ditched him and thought I would never see him again."

Ricki surely didn't offer details about her indiscretion with a complete stranger. However, Daniel was suspicious over her body language. He turned and glared at Kent, who returned a belligerent smile.

20

THE WITHDRAWALS

The thugs blindfolded Ricki and drove her to her house. A big guy walked around to the passenger door and led her by the elbow to her front porch. There were still splinters of wood from the break-in.

"Now wait two minutes after I leave before you remove your mask," the man warned.

Ricki waited, and then removed her blindfold and walked into the house. It was time to call her financial institutions.

Since the new JTST investments are in pending status, Ricki started with the next one on the list—Jefferson Woodward Wealth Management in Amelia. She tapped the number and it rang twice, three times, and someone finally picked up on the fourth ring. A pleasant woman answered, "Jefferson Woodward Wealth Management, Sarah speaking. With whom do I have the pleasure of speaking?"

"Hello, my name is Ricki Valentes and I have a brokerage account." She was asked to confirm the last 4 digits of her SSN, followed by a secret security question that was on file. "What was the name of your first pet?"

"Heidi, my dog."

"That's correct. I have accessed your account. How can I help you today, Ms. Valentes?"

"I would like to liquidate the account. I have a wire number for you when you're ready."

"Oh, sorry to lose you as a customer. Was there something that we at Woodward could've done better?"

"No, I was satisfied. I just need to handle some other priorities."

Ricki read the number that LD wrote on the wire instructions. Sarah completed the screens and tapped enter. *One million dollars transferred somewhere out of the country! Gone! Poof! Damn, that was too quick!* Ricki thought.

Seconds later, the representative texted the transaction receipt to Ricki and the process was complete.

Ricki skipped the credit union for now and called Wildwood First Federal. Same routine. Ricki said please liquidate my account and wire the money to the account number that I will provide. The representative was Mrs. Lewis. Seconds later, four million was on its way. *This is way too easy!*

Finally, it was time for the Zuberg National Credit Union. Then Mrs. Witherington came on the phone again. "Ms. Valentes, you said that you want a withdrawal of one million dollars, correct?"

"Yes, that's right."

The representative came back on the line and said, "I'm sorry, we have a new regulation here at the credit union. Any withdrawals over seven-fifty require you to come in person and sign a legal form. Can you come down to the credit union? We'll have you out of here in twenty minutes if all goes well."

"Oh, I see," Ricki groaned. "I'll be there in half an hour."

———

Ricki pulled her Mustang into the credit union's parking lot. She threw it in park, grabbed her portfolio on the seat, and headed toward the entrance. She walked to the information desk and asked for Mrs. Witherington.

"She's with another customer," the young woman at the information desk said. "But she'll be wrapping it up in a few minutes. In the meantime, can I bring you water?"

"That would be great," Ricki said. The woman handed her a bottle of water and asked her to be seated in the lobby.

Ten minutes later, the manager wandered over to see Ricki. "Well hello, Ms. Valentes," Mrs. Witherington said. "I'm sorry for making you come down here, but you know the intricacies of banking rules."

I don't know or care about the rules of banking. I just want my damn money so I can save Daniel's life from prickface, LD!

She led Ricki to the right side of the lobby and down the hall to the administrative offices. "Please have a seat."

Ricki sat and looked around at Mrs. Witherington's credentials on the wall.

"I see that you're making a substantial withdrawal today," Mrs. Witherington said.

"Yes, I'm considering buying a new home in Indian Hill. I'm pooling my funds for the transaction," she lied.

"Good for you, Ms. Valentes. I bet it's quite exciting, purchasing a new home." Ricki looked around some more. *Why must I explain to this strange woman why I want my money? Should I tell her the truth, that I am being extorted by some asshole named LD who is part of a huge crime syndicate? And that this money will be wired to an offshore shell company in God knows what country? And that any moment he could be killing my boyfriend and soon-to-be husband if I don't get the money quick enough?*

———

After Ricki signed the document, Mrs. Witherington walked toward the copy room. While she was making the copy, she waved to her co-manager.

"Hey, Marjorie. I have a client, Miss Valentes, who is liquidating her million-dollar account."

"Wow, that's a big one."

"Yes, and she's looking around the room and appears to be nervous about something. Who would be nervous about a big withdrawal?"

"Sounds strange."

"Agreed. Come over and see if you notice anything."

———

Mrs. Witherington returned to her office with two copies of the form. "Ms. Valentes, this is Marjorie Taylor who will serve as the second notary."

The two women shook hands.

"Hello," Ricki replied.

"Please sign each form at the X."

Ricki signed the documents and laid down the pen. While Ms. Taylor was pulling out her notary stamp, she noticed that Ricki was shaking her leg under the table and glancing around in the room.

Marjorie elbowed Mrs. Witherington gently and motioned with her a head nod. Mrs. Witherington noticed it as well but continued talking.

"Well, that does it for the paperwork."

Ricki sat motionless as she worried about Daniel. "Ms. Valentes," Mrs. Witherington began. "Is everything okay?"

"Huh, oh I'm sorry. Yes, it's quite okay. I've had a very long day, that's all."

"Alrighty, then. I'll be back in a few."

More time for Ricki to ponder her situation. *I won thirty-nine million from the lottery and it's been nothing but trouble. From the time I collected the windfall, people have scouted me on the phone, showed up at my door as old friends, begged for money, beaten my door down, kidnapped me, beaten my boyfriend, and now they're outright stealing the money! And oh, by the way, my boyfriend is being held hostage until I deliver the money to that creep, LD!*

Mrs. Witherington returned ten minutes later and confirmed that the wire had been processed.

"Here is your Confirmation of Wire Transfer."

"Thank you very much," Ricki answered with a fake smile. *Easy come, easy go!*

————

Returning home, Ricki believed that her mission with the financial institutions was complete. She heated some spaghetti and meatballs and ate slowly. Her head pounded and her thoughts wandered. *I must get my life back together…I need normalcy. Screw the lottery money. I was just fine without it!* Thoughts of the windfall gave her a terrible headache.

She washed the dishes and continued to brainstorm on her path forward. At 5:45 her cell rang. She hoped it was someone from LD's gang.

"Hello?"

It was LD himself. "Good job, Ricki. You passed the test."

"I know I did. Now give me Daniel back!"

"Hey, hey. Don't forget, little darling. We're still in charge here!" LD boasted. "We'll drop him off at your house in an hour."

"Thanks," Ricki said. The phone went dead.

———

At 6:50, Daniel was dropped off by LD's goons and was forced to walk the final three blocks to Ricki's house. LD didn't take any chances. Daniel's right leg was still heavily bandaged from the gunshot wound in the woods and both sides of his face were swollen.

"Thank God, you're home," Ricki yelled as she jumped in his arms. They hugged and kissed.

"I love you, honey," Daniel replied. "I feel so bad about your lost money."

"Screw it! At least we still have the 30 million in JTST," Ricki said.

"Yeah," Daniel agreed, "I wonder what's the latest on Jeremy? Is he still in a coma?" Daniel went back to the bedroom and grabbed his backup cell. LD had confiscated his primary cell. "Darn, it's dead."

Daniel plugged in the power cord and Googled "Jeremy Staymour coma." The first result said:

Jeremy Staymour won a soccer all-star tournament in the UK.

Wrong guy. He scanned a few entries down and it read:

Cincy Man Awakens from Lengthy Coma.

Bingo. Daniel scanned the article. "It says he awakened a few days ago. Good thing LD didn't get word of this or he may have held me there until he got the rest of the money!"

———

FBI agent Lewis Rolfes investigated international financial crimes for ten years. Most recently, he had been investigating a case through FBI agents covering the Dark Web. He discovered that some unusual banking transactions were coming out of Argentina. The FBI had planted a mole deep in the financial sector.

Some of the agents suspected an underground stock exchange operating through the Dark Web. They just had to confirm it via a major bust. The mole was able to gather some interesting transactional information when he hacked into the crooked organization's server. Dozens of transactions were made between Argentina SE Roberta and Evina and a US company called Evergen Magnetta. FBI agents investigating Evergen spotted a man visiting the company one year ago. After some research, the agents determined the man was Jeremy Staymour. Turns out Staymour discussed business possibilities with Evergen.

The FBI monitored Staymour and his company, JTST Investments. The agency suspected foul play but was never able to prove anything.

Agent Rolfes did an FBI search on Staymour and found three links:

Man shot during drive-by shooting on Fountain Square
Woman jogger performed CPR
Investment Manager in a coma.

Agent Rolfes turned to one of his subordinates. "Let's book a flight to Cincy."

21

FBI WANTS ANSWERS

Rolfes and another agent walked through the lobby of County Memorial Hospital. They were accompanied by local police Detective Lankford who had been working the Staymour case for months. The FBI had contacted Lankford but had not yet told him what they knew about Jeremy. *Here we go,* thought Lankford. *This is the point where the feds barge in and take over the investigation.*

All three men stepped into the elevator and pushed the button for Staymour's floor. Wanting to break the ice, Lankford spoke first.

"What FBI office are you guys from?"

"I'm out of Chicago," said Agent Rolfes, "and Agent McKinney is out of the regional office."

"Okay, nice to meet you guys," Detective Lankford said, extending his right hand. As they shook hands, they stepped into the elevator and Lankford led them to Staymour's room. Nurse Curtis greeted them and they flashed their badges.

"Agent Rolfes and this is Agent McKinney, and I guess you know Detective Lankford."

"Yes, we do," Nurse Curtis confirmed.

The two agents and Lankford walked over to Jeremy's hospital bed.

"Hello. You must be Jeremy?"

"Hello." The men introduced themselves and shook hands. Nurse Curtis left the room to allow privacy.

Jeremy had a tightening in his stomach over what he feared was coming next.

"Mr. Staymour, you probably know why we're here." Agent Rolfes began. Then he paused for a few seconds for emphasis but Jeremy didn't bite.

"No, how can I help you?"

Rolfes continued. "Our investigative team along with the SEC have discovered that you were involved in some unusual international trades—specifically transactions with an Argentina Exchange that can only be contacted via the Dark Web."

Jeremy looked up but didn't answer.

"Have you heard of a company called Evergen Magnetta?" Rolfes asked. Staymour had a blank look on his face and shook his head.

"Let me help you remember. Our agents spotted you entering the company about a year ago. Do you recall? Our sources have linked you with Larry Donners, who goes by LD, and his gang."

"Not exactly. Here is what happened," Jeremy began. "In July, I received an unsolicited call from a Mr. Stoneman from Evergen Magnetta. He asked if we were taking on any new clients…said he had about five million to invest."

"Okay, then what?" Rolfes asked.

"So I made an appointment with him sometime in mid-July. He shows up at my office and I ask him to complete our new client survey just so we could feel him out… to see if we could provide the service he was seeking," Jeremy said. He paused and then continued.

"He completes the survey and we discuss all the usual stuff—risk tolerance, short- and long-term goals, and investment choices, stuff like that."

Dawn from reception filled the agent's coffee cups during a pause in the conversation and they nodded in appreciation.

"So then what happened?" Rolfes asked as he sipped his coffee.

"Stoneman answered the prompts in the survey and everything moved along nicely. But then he changes the conversation and propositions me. Asks if I'd consider making a lot of money, as in millions or maybe tens of millions."

"Wow. Please continue," Agent Rolfes said as he jotted a few notes.

"He said that they needed an investment guy to run what he called 'some phony stock exchanges' in Argentina and a few other countries. I had no idea what he was talking about, so I cut him off immediately when he hinted at illegal transactions, fraud, extortion, and who knows what else."

"Interesting," Rolfes responded. "Then what?"

"I didn't appreciate the fact that he came in under false pretenses so I asked him to leave. I escorted him to the door and told him to never come back."

"So why are you smiling?" Rolfes asked.

"Well, in Mr. Stoneman's zest to get me on board with his plan, he slipped and told me a little too much. He told me that the operation was called 'Smokestack' and later in the conversation, he accidentally told me that the scheme involved illegal investing internationally and illegal betting of race cars. He said that drivers were throwing races in an illegal betting scheme."

"Interesting. So that would change the gambling winnings."

"Yes, this thing is massive and involves tens of millions of dollars," Jeremy said.

"Did he say anything else?" Rolfes probed.

"He started telling me other irregularities, but I cut him off, I didn't even want to know anymore. I just told him I was out. Not worth losing my license or going to jail."

"Who were his partners?" Rolfes asked.

"He mentioned the name Donners as the ringleader and some guy named Kinsey as one of his assistants."

Rolfes looked up from his notes and told Jeremy some new information. "We were watching Kinsey, but one day, he fell off of our radar. Not sure where he is. Just disappeared."

"Interesting," Jeremy said.

"Please continue," Rolfes directed.

"Well, I told you my meeting with Stoneman was on a Friday afternoon? I saw on the net that he was found with his throat slit that same evening."

"Okay," Rolfes said as he looked up from his notepad. "How does this connect to the drive-by shooting?"

They were interrupted by a woman who refilled their coffee. Then Jeremy took a sip and continued.

"When I saw the news of Stoneman's murder, I didn't sleep too well that night. So Saturday morning I came to the office to catch up on my caseload of new clients."

"Then what?"

"After working for about half an hour, I glanced out my window. Two men watched me through binoculars from another office building beside mine."

"Okay, can you just tell me what happened," Rolfes asked impatiently.

"I continued working and tried to ignore them for about ten minutes. When I swiveled my chair, I saw one of the men hide behind a curtain when he thought I spotted him. Then my cell rang. When I answered, a man shouted, 'Staymour, you're a dead man!' That's when I slammed my laptop closed and stormed to the elevator. I ran through the lobby and bolted. There were loads of people on the Square. It must've been an early Convention."

"Then what?"

"I looked around and heard the screeching of a BMW racing toward me and I saw guns aiming out the window. Then I heard pop, pop, pop."

"Sounds like quite an ordeal. Then what?" Rolfes asked.

"I felt a severe stinging in my neck and arm. My vision faded and I thought I might die. And that's all I remember."

"Do you remember the woman jogger?"

"No, everything was foggy, I can't remember any of it," Jeremy said. As he tried to pick his brain to remember more, everything got foggier for a few minutes. He stared upward then shook his head in an attempt to clear his mind.

"Do you remember anything while you were comatose?" Rolfes asked. Jeremy didn't answer.

Noticing that Jeremy was suddenly struggling, Rolfes spoke again. "Excuse me, Mr. Staymour?"

"Oh, I'm sorry. I'm still a little woozy. What did you ask?"

"What do you recall while comatose?"

"Most of the time, it felt like a deep sleep with darkness. But I did have strange dreams where nothing made sense."

"Interesting…well let's take a restroom break," Agent Rolfes said. "Then we can wrap up."

―――――

When the agents and Detective Lankford returned from the restroom, Rolfes resumed the conversation.

"Mr. Staymour, thanks for clearing that up. I have just a few more questions."

"Okay, go ahead."

"Mr. Staymour, how do you explain your signature on four stock certificates from Mexico and one from Argentina?"

"That must have been forged," Staymour shot back directly but rather politely. "As a CFP, I must abide by strict ethics rules."

"I understand. But we show your name on the Argentina stock transfers," Rolfes shot back.

"All forged and counterfeit!" Jeremy responded.

"Okay, we'll look into that. But we believe this caper may involve up to five other countries, maybe more," Agent Rolfes confirmed from his notes.

Noticing a lull, Agent Rolfes continued speaking to Jeremy.

"We have been watching Donners and Kinsey for a year, but so far we don't have enough to nail them. We have a strong suspicion that Donners and several other men are tied in with international dark web investors."

Then Rolfes continued. "Donners is very clever and always covers his tracks."

Jeremy rubbed his eyes, looked over, and said, "Agent Rolfes, I'm feeling very tired and I need to get some sleep."

"Okay, Jeremy. I'll wrap this up quickly. In the light of events and to clear your name, Mr. Staymour, would you be interested in participating in a sting operation to entrap LD? We'll bring down his operation once and for all."

Jeremy rubbed his chin as he pondered his answer. He looked at Agent Rolfes and said, "Based on what I just told you, I'm free of any criminal wrongdoing, correct?"

"That's right. I'll forward your testimony to the SEC, but I can't promise anything. You would be volunteering your support to the Government based on your own free will."

"Well, I have a few weeks of mandatory rehab here at the hospital," Staymour mentioned.

"We understand. The sting won't happen overnight."

"Okay, deal," Jeremy said. When he was sure his name was clear, he agreed to the sting.

Both FBI agents and Detective Lankford seemed to be satisfied. Agent Rolfes spoke last. "Thanks for your statement. We'll be in touch, Mr. Staymour."

All of the men shook hands and said their goodbyes. The FBI agents and Lankford gathered their notes and left the hospital. Ten minutes later, Jeremy fell soundly asleep.

———

Jeremy completed his rehab schedule on Day Twelve. It was earlier than expected but he was cleared to be discharged from the hospital. Because of the long coma, he would have to attend therapy and follow a strict exercise schedule at home for six weeks.

Nurse Curtis rolled Jeremy in a wheelchair down the hall where he received high fives from the doctors and a few patients that he met. Nurse Curtis rolled him to the elevator and then through the lobby to a waiting car. The driver was his sister, Liz, who hopped out and circled the car to help Jeremy climb in.

"It was nice getting to know you guys," said Nurse Curtis. "It's always great to see a positive outcome for coma patients. That was scary, Mr. Staymour!"

"Sure was. And you're welcome, Nurse Curtis," Jeremy said. "I'm glad I brought a little excitement to the boring hospital routine!"

"Ha, ha. You SURE did!" the nurse said as she patted him playfully on the shoulder.

Liz chimed in. "Thanks for taking such good care of my brother. He couldn't have done it without you!"

"I slept through most of it," Jeremy kidded. "But thanks, Nurse Curtis, for keeping me alive!"

"You're certainly welcome. And I don't want to see either of you back in the hospital for a long time. Be safe!"

Liz drove away slowly and turned left on the entrance ramp to the highway.

22

A LITTLE FOR YOU,
AND A LOT FOR ME

Two weeks later, Jeremy drove to work in his Porsche Boxster for the first time in over six months. The windows were open and his sandy hair was blowing in the breeze. He was replaying in his mind the conversation with Agent Rolfes from the FBI. He couldn't wait to entrap old man LD. Lock him up and throw away the key!

The two lanes on the right were *Kentucky-Only* lanes, so Jeremy stayed in the left two lanes. He traveled about another mile through some orange construction barrels, but at least the traffic kept moving.

He exited left on Fifth Street and cruised to the stoplight at the end of the exit ramp. To the left of Jeremy's car was a rather disheveled homeless man holding a cardboard sign.

While the light was still red, Jeremy grabbed a bill out of his wallet, and then crumbled it up into his fist. Then he held his closed fist out the window.

The curious man came over to the Porsche and said "Hello, sir."

"Hi there. Can you guess what's in my hand--a ten, twenty, or fifty?"

The man scratched his head and said, "Let's go with Fifty."

Jeremy opened his hand and it was a fifty-dollar bill. He handed it to the man as his prize.

"Thank you so much, sir! This is unbelievable!"

Jeremy smiled at the man and thought to himself. *Wow, that sure puts things into perspective. The poor guy just received a windfall!*

A few blocks away was the luxurious downtown office building. Jeremy walked through the lobby and recalled his last trip down the elevator. At least the building added additional security guards and additional high-tech electronic security since the shooting.

"Hi William."

"Welcome back, Jeremy."

"Thank you, thank you. Great to be alive and breathing."

When he entered the suite, he greeted Marie and a few other staffers. They were glad the boss was back to work. Everyone migrated to the vending area to discuss their families. Then Jeremy shared a few stories about the lengthy coma.

As he walked toward his office, Jeremy got Marie's attention.

"Excuse me, Marie? Can we push through the pending trades since I'm back in the flesh?"

"I've already called the Government Rep because I knew you were coming in today. I'll let you know when they call back."

"Thanks, Marie. You're the best!"

Before the shooting, Jeremy had lunch with Daniel Flarity and his millionaire girlfriend. As the result of their discussion, Jeremy planned on a 70/30 split. Seventy percent in stocks, thirty in bonds would be the proper allocation. The bonds would act as a safety net.

After Jeremy's discussion with Agent Rolfes, the feds were satisfied with Jeremy's story that he was not a criminal and that he was running from what he uncovered. In addition, Jeremy was helping to expose and capture LD and the gang. So the government unfroze JTST's investments that were in limbo. Jeremy smiled as he tracked the list of trades on his monitor. The largest transaction was from Ricki Valentes.

———

Ricki received a notification on her cell that read:

Ricki Valentes – Investments confirmed…10:38 AM 2022 10.10
Total invested is $30,502,000

Ricki was relieved the transaction was complete. *The lottery winnings are finally invested!* But then she had a second thought. *How long until LD finds out? Jerkface will want his money too!*

———

Ricki's cell rang causing her to freeze. Two rings…three rings. *Do I have to answer? Do I want give thirty million to LD?* It rang a fourth time, so she had to answer.

"Hello?"

"Hello, Ms. Valentes? My name is Agent Rolfes with the FBI office in Chicago."

Ricki hesitated because she was expecting LD's call, NOT the FBI.

"Ms. Valentes," Agent Rolfes began, "we have been investigating Jeremy Staymour and his business for over two years. This includes the time before and after his coma. Our research concludes that Mr. Staymour is in the clear from any perceived business deals with international countries such as Argentina and Mexico."

"He is?" Ricki asked. "That's good, right?"

"Yes, Ms. Valentes. But even though Staymour is in the clear, he has agreed to join our sting operation to capture LD. Could you help us as well?"

There was silence on the other end.

Rolfes broke the silence. "If you accept, may I tell you what we need you to do?"

"Uh, sure."

"Okay, thanks. We have bugged LD's cell phones. He'll try to extort your JTST funds soon. I assume you know what that means?"

"I sure do! He beat up my boyfriend, Daniel, and threatened further harm unless I cooperated. He forced me to liquidate the three smaller accounts totaling six million dollars."

"—Oh, that was the part I was missing," Rolfes interjected. "Your boyfriend was being detained? Is his last name Flarity?"

"Yes, and now that JTST is back in business, I'm sure LD will be on the warpath for the other thirty million."

"You've got that right," Rolfes agreed. "I imagine he'll be calling today or this evening."

"Do me a favor?" the agent continued, "When LD tells you to wire the thirty million, stall him…slow roll him…tell him you have to visit JTST to countersign more paperwork. This will give our people time to contact JTST and give them a heads up and provide direction."

There was a pause, then Rolfes continued. "The liquidation of your thirty million dollar JTST account will be a complete fabrication, meaning LD and his thugs will get nothing."

"Good news," Ricki replied.

Then Rolfes spoke again. "We're dealing with a money-hungry madman named Larry Donners! If he senses the smallest slip-up, bullets will fly, and blood will pour. He has slaughtered his people for failing on a mission! He's a low-life intimidator with zero compassion for other humans! We know for a fact that he has mentally abused one of his associates, Kinsey. We believe he's beaten some of his henchmen for misdeeds."

"Wow, what a creep!" Ricki said.

"Yes, Ms. Valentes. You're the one who can stop him."

"Lucky me," she replied sarcastically.

————

Two days later, there was still no phone call from LD. Did the old man fall off the face of the Earth? Fat chance.

Ricki was caught up with housework, so she sat down and grabbed a fiction book from the coffee table. The first thirty pages went by quickly. Still no phone call, so Ricki flipped some more pages. The protagonist was running and ducking from a hail of bullets. Ricki turned the page and her phone rang.

"Shit! I wasn't prepared yet."

She took a deep breath and answered. "Hello?"

"Ms. Valentes?"

"Yes, this is she."

"Hi, it's LD. You probably knew I'd be calling."

"Well as a matter of fact, no. I was reading a book and the villain in the story is worse than you, if you can believe that!"

"Ha ha, that's a good one. Too bad this is real life!"

"Oh, so this is your idea of real life, huh? Stealing from everybody you can get your hands on!" Ricki shot back firmly. "Slap a few folks around, and even kill a few here and there if things don't quite go your way?"

At this point, she figured, what did she have to lose? She prayed that the FBI would be true to their word and that her account would be protected.

"Okay, okay I get your point, but let's get on with it," LD began. "I'm not holding anyone hostage this time, but I do know where your parents live, dear old George and Betty. Such fine parents."

"Okay…now you crossed the line, you creep! If you touch one hair on my parents' heads, I'll track you down and murder you in your sleep!" Ricki shouted. She had to put on an act so LD wouldn't be suspicious.

"Nothing will happen to them," LD said, "because I'm sure you'll do exactly as I tell you, just like the last time."

"Oh, Jesus! What is it this time?" she screamed into the phone.

"You have $30,502,000 parked at JTST. Since I'm a nice guy, the $502,000 is yours. The thirty million needs to go my way."

"That's so kind of you, LD," Ricki answered sarcastically. "At least you're not throwing me on the street!"

"Ha, I'll ignore that," LD said. "Here is the way I need the thirty million:"

> *$20,000,000 wire transfer to the same account as before.*
> *$5,000,000 in cash*
> *$5,000,000 in diamonds*

"And I need it in seventy-two hours, no longer. That'll give you time to purchase the diamonds. And remember, no funny business. I want your parents to live a very long life."

"So do I! And you better not hurt them!"

"I'll call you at the deadline," he said. There was a click and the line was dead.

———

Ricki called the FBI. She waited on hold for a few minutes as the call went through.

"Hello Agent Rolfes, it's Ricki Valentes. LD just called me and spelled out his demands."

"Okay. Let's add Jeremy Staymour to the call."

"This is Jeremy."

"Okay, Mr. Staymour, I have Ms. Valentes on the line and she was contacted by LD. So what did he say, Ricki?"

"He told me to wire twenty million, pull five million in cash, and purchase five million in diamonds."

"Interesting," Staymour said. "The diamonds are purchased directly by the customer, but I have a vendor I can recommend. However, the diamond purchase usually takes forty-eight hours."

"Well, he gave me seventy-two hours before he kills my parents," Ricki answered in alarm. "So we can't have any slip-ups, guys! This jerk means business!"

"You're right," Rolfes said. "So Ricki, go ahead and play your role tomorrow morning—drive to JTST, request the wire transfer, make the withdrawals or trades, and withdraw cash for the diamonds.

I'll notify the SEC that everything is only for show instead of official transactions."

"Got it. The one thing I learned is that the account coding is disguised as domestic but still goes to the shell company," Ricki said.

Rolfes acknowledged and then added one more detail. "Jeremy, please give Ricki two identical money bags tomorrow—one bag with the cash and the other bag stuffed with weighted paper that resembles cash—just to fool the eye. The real cash bag is only there in case LD sniffs out the decoy and threatens to shoot up the place."

The FBI's plan had a decent chance of working. But only time will tell.

23

A WIRE, SOME DIAMONDS, AND CASH

The next morning at ten sharp, Ricki walked across Fountain Square and stopped for a few minutes to enjoy the enormous fountain. Then she turned and walked a block and entered a gorgeous high rise. She flashed her ID to the security guard.

"Where to?" the gentleman asked.

"JTST Investments."

"That's on twenty-two. The elevator is to your right."

"Thanks and have a good day."

Ricki went up the elevator. She was already familiar with the building since she and Liz had visited Jeremy's suite while he was still in the coma. Seconds later she was standing at JTST's office suite, where she pushed the business doorbell.

A pretty receptionist opened the door and accompanied Ricki to Jeremy's office.

"Mr. Staymour, Ricki Valentes is here to see you."

"Oh, thanks, Andrea." Jeremy rose and walked over to greet Ricki.

"It's a pleasure to finally meet you in person, Ms. Valentes."

"Please call me Ricki."

"Oh sure," Jeremy began. "Did Daniel mention that he and I have known each other for years?"

"Yes, he's told me a lot about you."

"Uh oh…all good I hope," Jeremy smiled.

"Well, most of it," Ricki kidded. They had a few more minutes of small talk and then Ricki resumed with more serious conversation.

"So, Mr. Staymour, I need to ask you something. I'm fascinated with comas and would like to hear about your experience. What was it like being in a coma for six months? Is it a big, dark sleep? Did you hear voices, and were you in any pain?"

"Wow, thanks for asking. The whole thing was surreal! I was walking across the Square and there were lots of people. I heard gunshots and then felt the burning of bullets. After that, it was like flickering movie frames. A flash of someone giving me CPR, someone pushing me on a gurney with lots of confusion, and then lots of beeps in a large, dark room. And then I fell into a really deep sleep with a few strange dreams mixed in."

"Sounds bizarre," Ricki said. "But I'm glad you're back amongst the living."

"Thanks," Jeremy said. "Say, I have a meeting coming up so let's see if I have this straight. You're here to do some 'trades' and you need four items: a bogus wire receipt for twenty million, a bag containing five million in cash, raw diamonds worth five million, and a decoy cash bag, right?"

"That is correct," Ricki confirmed. "The twenty-million-dollar transfer is a bogus transaction to fool LD. So as long as we don't get our asses shot, we're good!" she joked.

"Yeah, let's not forget that!" Jeremy said. "I've already been shot once by that group! Now, what is the bogus account number for the wire?"

Ricki pulled out a note from her purse and read the number to Jeremy. This was the same spurious account number that LD gave her for the previous wire transfers that successfully fooled U.S. computers and the funds ended up in another country. Jeremy keyed the account into his laptop and added a tiny QR Code to tipoff the government channels as instructed. Jeremy sold twenty million in ETFs for the phony transaction.

Next he sold various investments totaling five million in cash.

Then Jeremy told her, "The diamonds will take forty-eight hours, so Wednesday morning at ten AM." Jeremy looked up and said "We'll have all of the items ready that morning. That's still within the window that LD gave you, right?"

"Yes, we made it by one day."

"Oh, one more thing, Ricki. I'm curious to know something. How crazy was the lottery experience?"

Ricki laughed and answered sarcastically. "Well, I was in shock when I won. But as you might expect, everyone comes out of the woodwork hoping to get a slice of the pie. Surprising how many people are your best friends, past and present." She paused a few seconds to reflect. "Money is a giant magnet to creeps like LD, a man I never cared to meet. I'll see you Wednesday."

———

When Ricki left JTST, she returned to her car and tapped a number in her cell. "Hi, Agent Rolfes, it's Ricki."

"Hello, that was quick. Did it go well?"

"Yes. The twenty million in trades went through, and I have the phony receipt. The five million in cash will arrive tomorrow morning. I'll have one bag containing the cash and an identical bag with the phony dollar bills. The diamonds will be here Wednesday at ten."

"That's great," Rolfes said. "I'll have a Brink's truck at JTST on Wednesday at 10:30 AM. Thanks for all of your good work."

"You're welcome. And by the way, the drop-off location is at the Old Rusty Cavern, five miles south of Bellevue on Rural Route 5," Ricki said.

"Got it. And we'll have about five or six fully armed FBI agents looking for action!"

24

SHOWDOWN AT THE CAVERN

It was Wednesday afternoon, time for the official exchange of money, investments, and diamonds. The drop-off location was the Old Rusty Cavern in Kentucky. The crew consisted of LD, Bobby Wainwright, Kent Spreewell, and Stokely. Kinsey was on the run and hiding. No one had seen him in weeks.

Everyone in the gang except Kinsey arrived early in two black Cadillac Escalades. Fifteen minutes later, a large Ford F-350 Truck and a Brinks truck headed down the rural road toward the Cavern. Rolfes and other agents peered at a distance through the sights of some long-range rifles. Ricki and Daniel sat in the car and waited. Two men disguised as plainclothes cops were in the back seat.

"Where the hell's LD?" Ricki asked Daniel.

"No clue. Did he show up for the party?"

"That chicken-shit!" Ricki blurted out.

All four doors on the first Escalade opened in unison. Two big burly men hopped out of the rear doors and immediately assumed firing position toward Ricki's truck.

Then LD and Stokely stepped out of the front seats and proceeded slowly toward Ricki's truck.

Ricki and Daniel slid out of the vehicle and walked slowly and cautiously. Soon they were within fifteen feet of LD and Stokely.

"Do you have the stuff that we demanded?" LD yelled over.

"Yes, we do," Ricki answered.

"Okay, I assume it is in the Brinks truck behind you?"

"Yes," Ricki said.

"How many men are in there?"

"Two."

"Tell them to unload the items slowly and set them on the side of the truck," LD demanded firmly. His backup thugs shuffled forward and kept their rifles pointed intently at Ricki and Daniel.

Ricki leaned closer to the walkie-talkie on her collar. "Stack the boxes outside the truck."

Two armed guards carefully stacked three security boxes of cash side-by-side on the ground. The box nearest to the thugs contained the fake currency worth the price of a ream of paper. There was one crate full of custom-cut diamonds worth five million. The final box contained the receipt for the wire transfer (which Ricki hoped was phony).

"Now move away from the boxes, I mean get WAY AWAY!" LD screamed. When the Security Truck officers moved away, two more men stepped out of LD's truck and all six of them started advancing toward the boxes.

"Shoot now, fire!" Agent Rolfes yelled into his radio. Kent Spreewell was struck in the leg and then he was hit in the forehead. There was a barrage of bullets flying everywhere.

Two goons threw three smoke bombs near the security truck and the nearby boxes. Suddenly it was complete chaos. The FBI agents were still shooting from a distance but missing the culprits because of the intense smoke in the area.

Ricki's security guards grabbed the box of diamonds and quickly heaved it back into the truck. Next they snagged the boxes that either contained cash or fake cash. One box was accidentally kicked under the truck and the other one had a broken lid.

Hundred-dollar bills blew out of the box. One of the security guards was hit by an FBI agent's stray bullet that accidentally ricocheted off a vehicle. When the other security guard was retreating to the truck he was struck by a bullet from LD's gun. Next, one of the plainclothes cops fired three shots, killing LD.

In the middle of all this smoke and gunfire, an unidentified man made a late appearance. The mystery man played hopscotch around the dead bodies. Then he peered through the smoke and spotted one of the money boxes on the ground by the truck. He ran over, scooped it by the handle, and sprinted away.

Amidst the gunfire and chaos, the unidentified man cleared the smoke unharmed. Like a warrior gripping his treasure, he dodged the hail of bullets and fled by car.

The FBI took a desperate shot at the fleeing vehicle, but the driver got away. When the dust had settled, the car pulled to the side of the road. Kinsey had re-surfaced and had a bag full of money. He worked his entire life to get to this point. No one was about to stop him now!

25

OPEN THROTTLE

Kinsey drove five miles north and continued on a road that paralleled the Ohio River. He continued for about a mile while formulating an escape plan. *What should I do, WHAT SHOULD I DO?!*

He swung into a parking lot and glanced at the water. It was a nice day with a handful of boats puttering around and jet skis racing by. Kinsey nervously grabbed the bag from the back seat, jumped out, and began walking. Like a scared deer running from hunters in a competition, he appeared tired, confused, and bewildered.

Blue lights flashed behind him and a helicopter towered overhead. He ran along the Ohio River for about a quarter of a mile then stopped for a few seconds to rest. He looked across the river at the Cincinnati skyline.

As Kinsey continued running, he soon approached the Roebling Suspension Bridge that connects Kentucky to Ohio. Then he saw three policemen climbing the steps of the bridge to get a better vantage point. Kinsey spun around searching for options.

The career criminal looked back down at the river and scanned the shoreline. To his surprise, he spotted a ski boat and some jet skis docked on the shore under the bridge. He scooted down a small ledge to the sandy shore and pointed his gun at the four young men sitting in their boat.

"Get out! Get out of the boat now, or I'll kill you!"

The scared young men climbed out and ran to the shore. Kinsey splashed through the knee-deep water and jumped in the boat. The engine started on the first try. He idled for a few seconds, turned the wheel, and pushed down on the throttle. Kinsey's getaway boat was storming downriver with no particular destination in mind..

Seeing Kinsey's escape, the officers ran to shore. At a closer look, one of the men was Detective Lankford. He and the policeman named Officer Potter hopped on the two jet skis and aimed them toward Kinsey's getaway boat.

———

Kinsey's decision to select the ski boat over the jet skis was not the best decision because both jet skis had a maximum speed of 70 MPH. Lankford and Potter opened up their throttles to only three-fourths tilt, and they gained substantially on Kinsey.

Noticing that his pursuers were closing in, Kinsey grabbed his revolver, turned, and shot in Lankford's direction. However, the bullets did not even come close to Lankford. Both jet skiers decided to hang back just a little to ensure they were beyond shooting range.

As the pursuit continued, the paranoid Kinsey turned and looked behind himself. "Back off you damn cops!" he screamed and he shot a couple more rounds at the policemen.

When Kinsey faced forward again, he was shocked at what he saw. Two gigantic cigarette boats were darting toward him at about 100 MPH!

"Jesus!" Kinsey yelled as he angled his boat sharply and nearly capsized it. He slowed down and recovered by turning left. Meantime, Lankford and Potter nearly caught Kinsey's boat.

Seconds later, Lankford decided to go for it. He accelerated his jet ski and reached the side of Kinsey's boat. Then he ducked another gunshot and climbed aboard the boat. Kinsey turned and pulled the trigger again but heard only a click.

"Dammit!" he yelled as he tossed the gun at Lankford striking him harmlessly in the shoulder.

———

Once aboard the boat, Lankford ran toward Kinsey and wrestled him from the steering wheel. The boat zig-zagged across the water as the men fought. Kinsey swung wildly, but Lankford ducked. Then,

Lankford landed a strong right and a left to the jaw. The men wrestled some more and then fell to the floor of the out-of-control boat.

Seconds later, Potter's jet ski was slowing to a stop and tapped into the boat, but he was still able to hoist himself aboard to help corral Kinsey. Detective Lankford lunged at the wheel and re-gained control of the boat before it struck a dock on the Cincinnati side of the river. Potter handcuffed Kinsey and read him his rights.

The cigarette boat pulled up slowly next to the policemen and their captive.

"Hello, gentlemen," Lankford said as he greeted them. The huge boat carried Rolfes and two other FBI agents.

"Nice day for a casual boat ride, huh gentlemen?" Rolfes said with a smile.

"Just my idea of fun!" Lankford smirked.

"And oh, Detective... did you happen to spot a bag of valuables from our friend, Mr. Kinsey?" Still lying handcuffed on the floor of the boat, Kinsey popped his head up and looked to the stern.

Detective Lankford walked back there and spotted the bag. He bent over, yanked the zipper, grabbed a large stack of dummy paper bills, and launched them high in the air. As Lankford watched the green paper squares float like confetti to the river, he turned to his nemesis.

"Hey Kinsey, isn't that beautiful...I hope it was all worth it to you. And most importantly, I hope you enjoy your windfall!"

EPILOGUE

AFTER THE SHOWDOWN

After the dust settled, the FBI fully investigated Jeremy Staymour and his testimony to Agent Rolfes was verified. As a result, Jeremy was cleared of any wrongdoing and each of his investment licenses remained in force.

Two months after the shootout at the Old Rusty Cavern, Jeremy met an elite sports agent who connected him with some high-salaried baseball players, hockey players, and golfers. Those portfolios averaged one hundred million dollars per athlete. Jeremy's selection of fancy cars improved drastically. His sister, Liz, completed her Real Estate license and planned on targeting the larger homes in the Cincinnati suburbs of Loveland and Indian Hill. She remained friends with Ricki and they met for lunch often.

All of the money that LD extorted from Ricki Valentes was recovered by the authorities. Two days later, Ricki's JTST investment accounts were completely restored. Ricki and Daniel traveled to Bali for an extravagant three-week vacation. Daniel was glad to have Ricki back, but he had doubts about her fidelity in the relationship. He often wondered if she had an affair with Kent Spreewell. Daniel was relieved, however, that Kent was killed during the shootout at the Cavern.

Detective Lankford took two weeks of vacation with his wife and daughter, Sara. They traveled to Destin, Florida for a much-needed beach vacation.

Kinsey was sentenced to up to 15 years for the attempted murder of Jeremy Staymour and up to 15 years for the attempted murder of Liz Staymour. He is also being investigated for at least five other murder cases that are currently unsolved. The authorities believe that the cases directly or indirectly involved Larry Donners, or LD.

———

Liz Staymour and her boyfriend, Heath Livingston, were sunbathing on their giant deck that overlooked a dense green forest. Liz sipped a decadent Yellow Tail wine and Heath enjoyed a scotch on the rocks. The mating calls of a dozen birds echoed through the trees.

Heath rubbed suntan lotion in circular motions on Liz's shoulders and back.

"Ouch, honey! I think my shoulder got fried yesterday at the lake," Liz said as she winced.

"Sorry, honey, can I fill your wine?" Heath asked.

"That would be wonderful. Could you bring me some ice in a glass?"

Heath nodded, then opened the sliding doors and headed for the refrigerator. While returning, he carried an ice bucket, a fresh bottle of Yellow Tail, and a tall-stemmed wine glass. Then he pulled the white monogrammed napkin from his shoulder and handed it to Liz.

"Thanks so much, darling," Liz said. "You're the best!"

"No, no, honey. It was all you. The way you were so patient and caring for your brother while he was in a six-month coma!"

"Well anyone would've done the same thing," Liz answered.

"Heath looked softly into her eyes and said, "You're so awesome."

Liz smiled at Heath's sudden flow of affection. Intimate conversations like that confirmed that Heath would someday be her forever prince.

"Hold that thought," Heath said. "I'll get the hors d'oeuvres." He rose and walked confidently to the kitchen and opened the oven door. Then he slipped on two large pot holders and grabbed the spinach artichoke dip. Upon closing the oven door, Heath felt his cell vibrate in his pocket. So he carefully set down the food dish and grabbed his cell. He recognized the New York caller, so he answered.

"Hello?"

"Heath, it's me," the rather deep voice began. "You alone?"

"Oh hi, Rocko. Yes, but just for a few seconds. I have company on the deck."

"Okay, I'll talk fast. I discussed it with Walterman, and he approved. You're the official replacement for LD"

Smiling brightly, Heath managed a few words. "Uhhhh, thanks, Rocky. I'm so honored by the news."

There was another pause, and then Rocky continued. "Well deserved, my boy. And Heath?"

"Yes sir?

"Keep a close eye on Staymour's sister." There was a click as the call ended.

Heath's heart pounding, he sat down for a minute to let the good news sink in. "I sure will," Heath whispered while pumping his fist in the air.

His world shining brightly, the new ringleader lit a cigarette, took a nice draw, and blew two perfect ovals.

Author's Note:

Dear Readers:

Thank you for delving into the world of "Windfall One." Jeremy Staymour and the gang truly appreciate your participation!

Background: I've always wondered how people would react if large sums of money were unexpectedly dropped in their laps. Would life remain normal or would it simply go off the rails? Would millions of dollars tempt them to act in strange or mischievous ways? Do good guys become bad guys? How soon do the bad guys go after the money? Ricki Valentes finds out after winning the lottery. I hope you enjoyed all of the characters as they bounced around their board game of life.

Writing Process: My journey of writing "Windfall One" began over ten years ago. I wrote the first few chapters and then I stopped writing. The story needed to be cultivated over time. As it turned out, waiting was the best course of action.

Choosing a Title: Originally, I spent a lot of brainstorming and titled the manuscript "Paydirt." As publication neared, I was concerned that some readers might confuse the title with a football story or a Finance book, so I changed it to "Windfall One." The next book will have some of the same characters and will be called "Windfall Two."

Acknowledgements: Thanks to all of my readers as well as friends and relatives who encouraged me to continue this project through completion.

Thanks to my wife, Lee Ann, who provided endless support. Thanks to an accomplished author, Tim Smith, who edited the manuscript, and provided encouragement as well.

Reader Connection: I love hearing from my readers. Feel free to reach out to my socials or email below:

Linktree: https://Linktr.ee/jeffross.author
Website: https://jeffross.my.canva.site
Facebook: www.facebook.com/jeffross99
Email: jeffross.author@gmail.com
X: https://x.com/jeffrossauthor
Instagram: https://instagram.com/jeff.ross.author

About the Author

Jeff Ross resides in Dayton, Ohio. He holds a degree in Business Finance from Eastern Kentucky University. Jeff spends the majority of his time writing mystery/thrillers. He has decided to turn *Windfall One* into a series. The second in the series will be published later in 2025.

Jeff has also written a children's series titled "The Adventures of Max & Penny." When he's not writing fiction, Jeff enjoys playing tennis and guitar. He and his wife, Lee Ann, enjoy vacationing in Europe and in the panhandle of Florida. They especially enjoy spending quality time with extended family, including six grandkids.

Request to the Reader

Countless hours go into writing, publishing, and marketing a work of fiction. If you are so inclined, please consider leaving an honest review of *Windfall One* on Amazon. This small action helps tremendously in landing the book in the hands of additional readers in the genre.

Made in United States
Cleveland, OH
25 August 2025

19740692R00111